D1796627

LOVE'S OBSESSION

LOVE'S MAGIC SERIES BOOK 11

BETTY MCLAIN

This book is dedicated to the unlucky ones who have had to deal with Obsessive love.
Obsession is not love. It is an illness. Being the focus of obsession is frightening.
The ones who break free are lucky. There are many who are not so lucky.

CHAPTER 1

oris Tims was strolling down the sidewalk in Rolling Fork. She was on her lunch break from her job at the coffee shop. The Gallery was next and, on a whim, she decided to go in. She spotted two girls looking in the magic mirror. Doris frowned. The last thing she needed was someone else thinking he was in love with her.

Doris walked around looking at the displays. She was enjoying the quiet. When she turned around, she saw the girls were gone and she was standing by the magic mirror. She looked down at the mirror, and the face of Officer Mark Black Feather appeared in the mirror. He looked back at her and smiled. Doris knew him because she had seen him at the coffee shop. They had never spoken to each other because one of the other waitresses always hurried to take his order.

Mark smiled at the familiar face in the mirror. He had noticed her before, but had not had a chance to get to know her. "Hello," he said.

Doris stood there, stunned. She did not know what to say. She just stood there looking at Mark.

"Are you alright?" Mark asked with concern.

Doris shook her head and, still without saying anything, hurried out of The Gallery. When she was outside, she hurried along the sidewalk in the direction of the coffee shop. Suddenly she heard the sound of a motorcycle engine racing. She looked up, startled. Derrick Bolin was riding his motorcycle on the sidewalk, and he was headed straight for her. Before she could do anything, she felt herself lifted and carried to the side away from the advancing motorcycle. Derrick drove back onto the road and roared away down the road. Doris had her face buried in the chest of her rescuer.

Mark Black Feather had been in the store next to The Gallery when he had looked into a mirror and saw Doris. When she reacted the way she did, he had hurried outside to see if he could catch her and see what was wrong. When he had seen the motorcycle headed straight for her, his heart was in his throat. He ran to grab her out of the way before she could be hit.

"Are you okay?" asked Mark leaning away and looking down at Doris.

Doris looked up and shivered. She stared into Mark Black Feather's concerned face and sighed. "Thank you for saving me. Derrick almost got me this time," she said.

"You know the person on the motorcycle?" asked Mark.

"Yes, it was Derrick Bolin. He saw me and decided he wanted me. I told him no. He would not take no. He started harassing me. I reported him to the police, but they could not do anything without proof. Then my parents were killed in a drive-by shooting. I know his gang was responsible, but I can't prove it. So again, nothing was done; now, he has decided if he can't have me, no one else will."

All the time she had been talking, Mark had held onto her

and listened. When she stopped talking, Mark took out his radio and called the police station.

"This is Officer Black Feather. I just witnessed an attempted vehicular homicide. A motorcycle tried to run down a young woman on the sidewalk in front of The Gallery. The rider of the motorcycle was Derrick Bolin." He went on to describe the motorcycle and give its tag number. "I want an arrest warrant issued for Bolin at once."

Doris watched in amazement as he returned his radio to his belt and smiled at her. "Do you think they will get him?" asked Doris.

"Yes, they will get him, but you are still in danger, and his gang members may come after you when they find out he has been arrested. You have to be kept somewhere safe until he is taken care of," said Mark.

"I can't go to a safehouse," said Doris scowling. "I have a sister and brother I have to take care of. If I disappear, the CPS will take them away from me. I may not be able to get them back."

"We will go and pick up your sister and brother, and I know just the place to take you where you all will be safe. We have to go by the police station first and sign the complaint against Derrick. A judge has to sign off on the warrant."

Mark took her arm and led her to his car. He was not on duty, so he was in his personal car. Doris let him help her into his car and sat quietly while he reached across and fastened her seat belt. Mark smiled at her for reassurance and hurried around and got into the drivers' seat.

After a quick stop at headquarters, where Mark quickly told his story and signed the proper papers, he led Doris back out to his car and headed for the school.

Doris went in and signed her sister and brother out. She

told the school there was a family emergency. She was waiting outside the office when Orin and Sarah appeared. She quickly explained they had to leave for a while and led them out to Mark's car.

She gave Mark her address, and he drove them by their house so they could pack some clothes and the kids could get their favorite toys. When Orin and Sarah were occupied with their packing, Mark drew Doris aside and told her to be sure and pack all of their important papers.

"If it is alright with you, I am going to have a couple of friends of mine come by and pack up your house and put everything in storage. It will take a while for Derrick to go to trial, and his friends will be looking for ways to intimidate you. They will ransack your house and destroy everything in it, and sometimes they will burn the house. If it is in storage, you will have your things when this is all over."

Doris looked up at him with tears in her eyes, but with a determined look on her face. "Thank you, Officer Black Feather. I appreciate all you are doing for me. Please have everything stored as soon as possible."

Mark took out his phone and called his cousins on the reservation. He made arrangements for them to come out at once and pack up the house and store it all in a storage shed at his folks' house. When he hung up the phone, he found Doris and her siblings finished packing and ready to go. Doris handed him the key to the door, and they started out to Mark's car.

While they were putting their stuff in the trunk of the car, two trucks stopped and Mark's cousins arrived. "Doris, this is Jamie Long Feather and his brother Silas. Fellows, this is Doris Tims and Orin and Sarah."

They all said hello, and Mark gave them the key to the

house. The brothers headed for the house, and Mark ushered everyone into his car. Orin and Sarah were in the back seat and Doris was in the front with Mark. Mark smiled at Doris and squeezed her hand before starting the car.

"I haven't even asked you where we are going," said Doris.

"Somewhere you will be safe and protected. I'm taking you to my folks on the reservation."

Doris looked startled. "Are you sure they won't mind?" she asked.

"They will be pleased to help. Now, why don't you call the coffee shop and tell them you have to go out of town on a family emergency," said Mark.

Doris flushed. "I forgot all about the coffee shop. I should have been back from my lunch break an hour ago." She quickly called the coffee shop and talked to the manager. After she hung up the phone, she leaned her head back against the seat and closed her eyes for a minute.

"Did they give you a hard time?" asked Mark.

"No, he told me they may have to fill my position if I'm away too long. I can understand. I have no idea how long it will take to have Derrick taken care of, and I have to make sure Orin and Sarah are not hurt by him or his friends."

"They will not hurt any of you," said Mark determinedly.

Doris smiled. She had hope. The first glimmer of hope she had seen since the death of her parents, and it was all because of Mark Black Feather. According to the magic mirror, he was her true love. So much had happened; she had pushed the magic mirror to the back of her mind. Now, since things had quieted, it popped back up.

She looked over at Mark. She saw him checking his mirrors. "What is it? Is someone following us?"

"I don't think so. I have been going a roundabout way, so I

could check on followers. So far, I have not seen any sign of anyone. I'm hoping we took care of things fast enough to keep the gang from being aware of our plans," Mark smiled reassuringly.

"Officer Black Feather," said Doris.

"Mark, please, Officer Black Feather is such a mouthful." Mark flashed another smile.

Doris smiled. "Mark, I am so glad you were there when Derrick tried to run over me. If not for your quick action, I would not have made it. Thank you."

"You don't have to thank me. I hope we have a chance to get to know each other, but I will not put any pressure on you, so relax."

Doris relaxed for the first time in a while and smiled at Mark. "I would like to get to know you better," she said.

Mark turned into the reservation and started toward the roads leading to his parents' home. It took about thirty minutes of driving on the reservation to get to the Black Feather family home. There were several children playing in the yard, and they all called out to Mark when they saw his car. When he got out, they came running, calling out, "Uncle Mark."

Doris exited the car and smiled to see Mark's interaction with his nieces and nephews. Orin and Sarah left the car and came to Doris's side. She put an arm around each of them and hugged them close.

Mark started toward them but stopped when an older lady came out of the house. He turned and hurried up to her, giving her a hug and greeting her. He quickly explained why he was there and how Doris and her siblings needed a safe place to stay.

"Good," said Daisy Black Feather. "Moon Walking told me to get ready for your lady and her family yesterday."

Mark shook his head and walked with his mother to where Doris, Orin, and Sarah were standing.

Daisy came right up to Doris and took her hand. "Welcome to our home. I have rooms prepared for you. We will keep you safe. You have nothing to worry about. Come in and I will get you settled."

Doris was so surprised she followed without question. When Mark started walking beside her, she looked up at him in question. "How did she know to have rooms ready for us?" she asked.

"Moon Walking told her to be ready yesterday," replied Mark.

"Yesterday, everything only happened today," said Doris.

Mark shrugged his shoulders. "Moon Walking always knows. We have all learned to pay attention when she tells us something needs to be done."

"Yeah, I have heard stories about Moon Walking. She is a legend in her own time," agreed Doris.

They reached the porch, and Doris reached back for Orin and Sarah to usher them inside. Mark entered with his arm around Doris's shoulder. He was trying to reassure her.

"Mom, this is Doris Tims. The youngsters are Orin and Sarah. Doris, this is my mom, Daisy Black Feather," said Mark.

"I am pleased to meet you, Miss Tims," said Daisy.

"Please call me Doris. I am very happy to meet Mark's mom," said Doris.

"I have fixed a room for you to share with Sarah. Orin can share with my grandson Joey. He is staying with us while his mother delivers his baby sister." Daisy led the way to the bedrooms. She left Orin in a room with a boy about his age and continued down the hall to another room with a large bed for Doris and Sarah.

"This is lovely," said Doris, looking around at the spacious bedroom.

"I am glad you are pleased," said Daisy looking very satisfied.

"It is a beautiful room. I am sure we will be fine here," said Doris.

They left their things in the room and went back to the living room.

"I am going to have to get back to town," said Mark. "I need to check on how things are going. I want to see if they have arrested Derrick yet."

"I was hoping you would stay for supper," said Daisy.

"Couldn't you call and check on how things are going?" asked Doris.

Mark looked down at Doris's anxious face and took out his phone. He went outside to call. Sometimes they did not get the best phone reception on the reservation. The front desk put him through to the Captain. "Michaels," James barked into the phone.

Mark smiled. "Black Feather," he said.

"Mark," said James in a far more pleasant voice. "What's going on? I heard you issued an arrest warrant for Derrick Bolin."

"Yes, I saw him try to run down Doris Tims with his motorcycle. Luckily I was able to get to her in time to stop him from hitting her. Do you know if he has been arrested, yet?' asked Mark.

"No, his gang is hiding him, but we will get him. Is Doris safe?" asked James.

"Yes, I have her and her brother and sister on the reservation. I don't want anyone else to know where they are at. I had everything in their house put in storage so the gang can't get to it." said Mark.

"I won't say anything to anyone, and I will make sure it is not in any of our records. Why don't you take a few days off and keep an eye on the situation. You can set up guards for them," said James.

"I think I will," said Mark. "By the way, Doris saw me in the magic mirror."

"I hope everything works out for the two of you." Mark could hear the smile in his voice.

"Me, too," agreed Mark as he hung up the phone.

Mark went back inside and smiled at Doris. "Derrick has not been picked up. His gang is covering for him, but we will get him."

"I hope so," replied Doris.

"The captain told me to take a few days off and look after you," said Mark.

"Good," said Daisy. "I will go and put supper on the table."

"Can I help?" asked Doris.

"No,' said Daisy, waving her hand. "You stay and keep Mark company. I do not want him in the kitchen until supper is ready. He always tries to sneak samples before meals."

Doris laughed and Mark made a face. "Mothers never let you forget anything," he replied.

"I know what you mean," agreed Doris. "My mom was the same way." She sobered as she thought about never having her mom tease her again.

Mark quickly came to her side and pulled her close for comfort. "How long has it been since the shooting?" he asked.

"It's been three months. It feels like yesterday. Sarah still has nightmares about it. She was inside the house when they drove by shooting. Mom and Alfred were getting the groceries out of the car. They never had a chance. If we are driving and a car backfires, Sarah will duck down and hide."

"It is going to take time. We have a very good person here on the reservation she can talk to. She has helped a lot of little ones when they suffer some trauma. Maybe she can help Sarah," suggested Mark.

"Maybe, we will see," agreed Doris.

She realized she was still standing with Mark's arms around her and eased back slightly. It felt so right to be held by him that she hated to move. She looked up into his face and smiled. Mark smiled back and, leaning forward, kissed her lightly on her forehead.

Doris sighed and, pulling away slowly, went over and sat on the sofa. She looked around and then got back up and started going around looking at pictures. Mark started following her explaining who was in the pictures. When they came to a picture of Mark as a little boy holding a large bat trying to play ball with his older brothers, Doris laughed out loud. Mark looked insulted at first, then he smiled at the first real laugh he had heard from Doris.

"You were adorable," she said.

"Yes, he was," agreed Daisy, coming into the room. "Call the children in for supper," she told Mark.

"I had better call Orin and Sarah," said Doris.

"They are outside playing with the others," said Daisy.

Doris smiled. She had not even noticed the children going out; she had been so involved with Mark.

Mark called, "Supper is ready," out the front door, and kids started piling in, bringing Orin and Sarah with them. They all headed for the bathroom to wash their hands without being told.

Mark came over and, putting his arm around Doris, guided her into the supper table. They all took their seats. Some of the kids made room for Orin and Sarah. Mark held his mom's chair and then seated Doris beside his chair.

All of the children bowed their heads and held hands as Mark said a brief prayer of thanks. They were a happy family enjoying a meal together.

CHAPTER 2

The next morning, Daisy was getting Joey ready for the school bus when there was a knock on the door. When Mark opened the door, he found Moon Walking there.

"Good morning, come in," said Mark with a smile.

Moon Walking graciously came inside and smiled at Doris. "I wanted to catch you early before the bus came. I have made arrangements for the young ones to attend class at the reservation school as observers. It will be good for them to be occupied, and all of the children can learn from each other," said Moon Walking.

Doris turned to Orin and Sarah. "Would you like to go to class with Joey?" Both children nodded vigorously. "Okay, I don't see why not, as long as you want to go," she said to the smiling children. Joey was smiling just as big as Orin and Sarah.

"I have their lunches here," said Daisy. She brought two more lunch boxes to give to Orin and Sarah. The children accepted them eagerly, and everyone hurried outside as the school bus blew its horn. Doris watched as they loaded onto the bus and waved from a window as the bus pulled away.

"Do not worry about them. I have instructed a counselor to meet the bus and be sure the children are okay. She will keep an eye on them throughout the day," explained Moon Walking.

"Thank you," said Doris.

"I want you and your family to have a pleasant time here with us. You are always welcome here with us. It is always a pleasure to have one of our own meet their true love," said Moon Walking.

"You believe in the magic mirror?" asked Doris.

"Of course, there are many mysteries in the world. We have to accept help when it is offered, even if the help comes in the form of a face in a mirror," explained Moon Walking.

Moon Walking took Doris's hand and squeezed it. "You will be alright. You will come out of your troubles stronger than ever. Mark Black Feather is your destiny. He will not let anything happen to you." Doris flushed slightly and glanced up at Mark, who was smiling at her. "Now I have to go. I want to welcome the newest member to our tribe. Mark, you can drive me to your brother's house to meet his new daughter," said Moon Walking.

"Sure," agreed Mark with a quick smile for Doris and his mother; he followed Moon Walking outside.

"Is she always like that?" asked Doris after Moon Walking and Mark were gone.

"Sometimes it is worse," said Daisy. "Sometimes she talks in riddles, and it is hard to understand what she is trying to tell us. She was very clear this time."

"Wow," said Doris. "I met the famous Moon Walking."

Daisy laughed and turned toward the kitchen. "I have breakfast on the table. With the kids and Mark gone, we can sit down and enjoy our morning coffee," she said.

Doris followed her with a laugh. "I guess some things are universal no matter where you live," she said.

Mark's brother, Logan, was sitting on the front porch as Mark stopped in front of his house and helped Moon Walking out of his car. Logan rose and came down to meet them with a big smile.

"Hello, Moon Walking," he said. He gave Mark a big hug,

"Are Willow and the baby okay?" asked Mark.

"Of course," answered Moon Walking before Logan could say anything.

Both men looked at each other with a smile and shrugged their shoulders.

"Come in and meet my new daughter," said Logan.

Moon Walking and Mark followed him inside. They quietly made their way to the crib where the baby lay. They did not want to disturb Willow, who was sleeping.

"She's beautiful," said Mark.

They all turned and went back out to the porch.

"You will have your hands full with her," said Moon Walking. "Be prepared to chase the braves away when she reaches her teens. She is not meant for a simple life. She has great things in store for her. Keep our little Camille safe," said Moon Walking.

"How did you know we were thinking about naming her Camille?" asked Logan. "Silly question, of course you would know." Mark laughed at Logan's disgruntled expression. "Just you wait," said Logan. "Your time is coming."

"I can't wait," said Mark.

Moon Walking smiled at the brothers and looked at Mark.

"You can drop me off at my home. Then, I will let you get back to your future," said Moon Walking.

Mark obediently held the car door for her and waved his brother goodbye as he drove her to her home. When he dropped her off, Moon Walking turned to him. "Don't forget to arrange extra security for Doris and her family," she said.

"Do you think they are in danger here?" he asked.

"Obsession sometimes finds a way. Be careful for all of your loved ones. Make sure they are aware of the danger. Even the little ones need to be aware of the danger. They need to know to ask for help if it is needed."

"Thank you, Moon Walking. I'll take care of everyone," he promised.

Moon Walking patted his shoulder. "I know you will," she said

Moon Walking went inside, and Mark drove to his parents' house. Before he went inside, he called the head of security on the reservation and explained the situation to him and asked for extra security for his family. The head of security agreed and Mark went inside feeling much encouraged.

Daisy wanted to go and see Camille, so Mark took her and Doris over to Logan and Willow's house. Willow was awake when they arrived, so the women were in the bedroom ooohing and aaahing over the baby. Mark and Logan went out and sat on the front porch. Mark explained the situation with Doris and let his brother know Doris was his mate.

"I am happy for you. I hope it all works out for you. She seems like a lovely person, and I think she will fit in well here," said Logan.

"I think so, too. I just have to get her past the present danger, and then I can court her proper," said Mark.

"Well, you have Moon Walking on your side. You have a head start on working things out," laughed Logan.

"Yes, I do," agreed Mark with satisfaction.

"When will Dad be back from his trip to the capital?" asked Mark.

"He should be back in about a week. He and the elder

were meeting with the Indian commission today and tomorrow. I hope they can get some results this time," said Logan.

"We can only hope," agreed Mark.

Their dad was a lawyer and represented the Indian nation before the legislative committee. He had made several trips to the capital before without getting satisfaction. The committee would make promises, but not follow through. The Indian nation had a plus on their side this time. They were being backed by the Black Foundation. When the Black Foundation talked, the committee listened. Maybe this time they would get results.

Daisy and Doris came out of the house. Doris wanted to get home before the school bus ran. Daisy and Willow had decided to let Joey stay with his grandma a couple of more days before returning home. Doris was glad Joey was staying. She knew Orin and Sarah would miss him when he returned home.

They arrived home as the bus stopped to unload the children. Orin, Joey, and Sarah left the bus and hurried over to Daisy and Doris. Orin and Sarah looked happier than Doris had seen them in months. They were all talking a mile a minute.

Daisy held up a hand for quiet, and they all stopped talking.

"I have snacks prepared for you. As soon as you have changed clothes and washed your hands, you may come to the kitchen."

"Yes, Ma'am," responded the youngsters running for the house.

Doris and Mark followed behind Daisy into the house. Mark laid his arm across Doris's shoulder as they walked. He waited to see if she objected. When she didn't, he left it there and guided her inside.

Doris was very aware of Mark's arm across her shoulder. It felt right being there. She was not going to object. His presence made her feel safe and happy. This was the best she had felt in a long time. She sighed happily.

Mark heard the sigh. He smiled. She would be his. It was meant to be. Moon Walking and the magic mirror said so.

As soon as the children ate their snacks, they went outside to play. They were joined by other boys and girls who lived nearby. Mark's sister, Dawn, lived about a mile from there and regularly dropped her three, two boys and a girl, off at her mother's when she went shopping. They loved playing at Grandma's and it gave their mother a break.

She dropped them off today because she wanted to go by and see the new baby. She waved at Mark as she dropped them off. He was outside keeping an eye on the children. Mark waved back and stayed on the porch, watching the children run around and play hide and seek.

Doris came out and sat on the porch with him. He reached over and put his arm around her and pulled her close. "Is anything wrong?" she asked, seeing his sober expression.

"I don't want to scare you. I just want to be sure there is no danger. Moon Walking told me to alert security to keep an eye open for any problems," said Mark.

Doris stiffened. "I don't want to bring danger to your family. Maybe we should go somewhere else."

"No," said Mark. He turned her and looked in her eyes. "You are my family, too. I will keep all of you safe. I have increased security and have alerted family members to keep an eye out. I will not let anything happen to any of you." He hugged her close and kissed the top of her head. Doris laid her face on his chest and enjoyed the feel of his arms holding her close.

The girls squealed and ran over to the porch, avoiding

some boys who were chasing them. Doris looked around at their smiling faces and felt truly blessed to have this man and his family care about her and her family. She looked up at Mark and smiled.

"Thank you," she said.

Mark smiled back at her. "Thank me for what?" he asked.

"For making me feel safe, for giving me back hope, and for making my sister and brother smile again."

"You're welcome," he said and kissed her lightly.

Doris licked her lips and savored his taste on her lips. Mark's eyes darkened as he watched her. Before he could kiss her again, his sister drove up and stopped. She was back from seeing the baby and was there to pick up her bunch.

She got out of her car and approached the porch to say hello before she picked the children up.

Daisy, hearing the car, came out to say hello.

"Dawn, this is Doris. Doris, meet my sister Dawn, the mother of the latest three to join our group," said Mark.

"I'm pleased to meet you, Dawn," said Doris.

"I'm happy to meet you, too," said Dawn.

"Are Willow and Camille doing alright?" asked Daisy.

"Yes, they are fine. Sleeping a lot, but they should be up and making a racket in a day or two," said Dawn.

"Good," said Daisy with satisfaction.

The phone could be heard ringing inside, and Daisy excused herself to go answer it. "It's probably your father," she said as she left.

Dawn looked at Doris sitting with Mark's arm around her and smiled.

Doris was so comfortable in his arms, she had not even thought about moving. It was okay with Mark. He wanted her to be comfortable in his arms. He wanted to keep her there forever.

"Well," said Dawn. "I need to round up my bunch and get home so I can have dinner ready when Hank gets home."

"It was nice to meet you, Doris," she said.

"It was nice to meet you, too," said Doris.

Dawn called her children and they came running. They were waving and calling goodbye to all the other children. The other children were waving back and calling goodbye, Orin and Sarah included.

Daisy came back outside to call everyone in to eat. "Your father will be home day after tomorrow," she told Mark. Her face was glowing.

Doris looked at Mark and wondered if, after years of marriage, they would still have the kind of love his parents had. The kind of love to make the face glow at the thought of seeing the other person. Mark smiled at her. It was as if he was thinking the same thing. Maybe they could have that type of marriage, if they married, she thought.

CHAPTER 3

The next day followed the pattern of the first day. The children were all up and ready for school when the bus came for them. Daisy, Mark, and Doris enjoyed a leisurely breakfast after the bus left.

While the women were clearing away after breakfast, Mark went outside to call the station and see if there were any updates about Derrick. The officer in charge said they had not located Derrick. The police had issued a city-wide alert for him and were getting a lot of calls. The calls had not produced any results as of yet.

"We'll get him. He can't hide forever. He'll get cocky and show himself, and then we will grab him," reassured the officer. Mark hung up the phone very dissatisfied with the lack of results.

One of his mother's friends came by to visit with her, so after saying hello, Mark decided to take Doris on a ride around the reservation to show her around. He drove her by the school and the sports complex, built by the Black Foundation. He pointed out a line of stores. The grocer was the busiest. It seemed to be shopping day for many of the ladies. They all waved at Mark and looked curiously at Doris.

They passed several security patrols. They also waved at Mark. Mark took her by a plot of land close to his brother, Logan. Another brother, Marcel, lived on the other side of Logan. Mark pointed out the undeveloped land to her; it was two acres. "When I decide to build, this is where I will build a home," said Mark.

Doris looked around at the vacant land. "It's a lovely spot," she said. "It's nice and close to Logan and Willow." She turned and smiled at Mark.

"Yes, it will be nice for our children to be close to each other," agreed Mark.

"How many children are we talking about?" asked Doris.

"I will leave it up to the Holy Spirit to decide," said Mark seriously.

"Uh-huh," said Doris. "I think the Holy Spirit can use a little guidance."

Mark laughed. "I was only teasing. I think three is a nice group, but I will be satisfied with however many I am blessed with."

"I guess you will," agreed Doris. "Especially if you are planning on me having anything to do with it."

"Oh, you are most definitely involved in my plans," agreed Mark with a smile. "After all, the magic mirror agrees we are each other's true loves. There will never be another for me."

Doris leaned over and offered him a kiss. He wasted no time taking her up on her offer. When he finally drew back, they were both breathing hard. Mark rested his forehead on Doris's forehead while catching his breath.

Mark sighed, "I guess we need to head back to Mom's and see if she needs anything."

"Yes," agreed Doris.

When they stopped in front of the house and got out of the car, Mark's phone rang. Doris went on inside, and Mark stayed outside to answer his phone. "Hello," said Mark.

"Hello, this is James Michaels."

"Hello, Captain, what can I do for you? Do you have any news?" asked Mark.

"Yes, we picked up Derrick Bolin," said James.

"Great," said Mark.

"Yes, but Miss Tims is still in danger. Derrick's gang has been harassing the people at the coffee shop where she worked trying to find her. She and her family need to stay hidden until we can stop them," James said.

"I will make sure she stays safe," agreed Mark. "How much time can I take off?"

"You have plenty of vacation time built up. I let it out you are dealing with a family emergency and would be out for awhile. I will let you know when you have to appear at Derrick's trial. I stood in for you at his arraignment."

"Thanks, James. I owe you," said Mark.

"Yes, you do. I'll blame you when Cindy thinks I need more time off," James laughed.

"How is Cindy?" Mark asked.

"She's doing fine. She is just anxious to deliver and hold our daughter," said James.

"You're having a daughter," said Mark. "Congratulations. Give Cindy my love and you take care of her."

"I will to both suggestions," agreed James. "Keep in touch and be alert."

They both hung up, and Mark went inside to let Doris know what was going on. "I just talked to Captain Michaels. He said they picked up Derrick Bolin," said Mark.

"Great," said Doris.

"The Captain said he would let me know when I have to testify against him," said Mark.

"How long before we can go home?" Doris asked.

"I don't know. The Captain said Derrick's gang has been harassing the people at the coffee shop trying to find you," explained Mark.

"Are you going to have to go back to work?" Daisy asked Mark.

"No, the captain told me to stay and take care of Doris and her family. He led the people at the station to believe I was dealing with a family emergency," said Mark.

"Good," said Daisy.

"Yes, very good," agreed Doris.

Mark smiled at her. "I am not going to let anything happen to you or your sister and brother."

Doris went over and hugged him. "Thank you," she whispered.

Daisy watched them with satisfaction.

They heard the bus coming outside. They went outside to talk to Orin, Sarah, and Joey.

"Hi, everyone," said Mark as the children came onto the front porch. "Could we talk for a minute before you get changed?" Mark asked. All three stopped and looked at Mark with smiling faces. "You know why we brought Orin and Sarah here for a while?" he asked.

"So we would be safe from the bad men," said Sarah.

Mark smiled and hugged Sarah. "Yes, Sarah, so we could keep you, your sister and brother safe from the bad men. We have one of the bad men in jail now, but his partners, other bad men, are still looking for you. We need you to let us know if you see any strangers around. Stay in groups and don't go off by yourself. If you have any problems, yell and ask for help. The teachers at the school will look after you. If anyone else tries to take you, call for help. We will take care of you. You are safe with us. Can you do this for me?" All three children nodded their heads.

"Okay, go get changed and get your snack so you can play," said Mark. All three children hurried inside. "I don't think they really understand," said Mark with a sigh.

Doris came over and gave him a hug. "Maybe some of it got through. They had to be warned."

Daisy patted his shoulder. "We will keep a close eye on them," she promised.

The next morning, Mark received a call about Derrick's trial. It was set for two weeks. He told Doris about the date, and they were both nervous about the outcome of the coming trial.

Daisy was excited and rushed around cleaning and cooking while she waited for her husband to return home.

Doris and Mark smiled to see her so excited. When they heard a car stop out front, they all went out to see who it was. It turned out to be Jamie and Silas Long Feather. They greeted everyone and then asked to speak to Mark. Doris and Daisy went back inside, leaving Mark to talk to his cousins.

"The head of security has asked us to man the gate and make people we don't know show ID before they come on the reservation. We have had some motorcyclists trying to enter. They were turned back, but our guards are spread thin, and the head of security is afraid they will try to find another way in," said Silas.

"Why are they coming here before the trial?" wondered Mark.

"It may be you they are after. You signed the complaint against their friend," said Jamie.

"You may be right," said Mark. "They may not know Doris and her family are on the reservation."

"Just in case you are wrong, the chief of security has sent two men to keep an eye on your home until this matter is settled," said Jamie.

"Thanks for letting me know. My dad is expected home today. If we have any problems, both he and I are excellent shots. If they come snooping around here, they may cease to be a problem."

"We will see you later," said Jamie. "Be safe." The brothers left, and Mark went inside.

The next car they heard was Mark's dad, Glen Black Feather. They all stayed inside so Daisy could greet him alone. When they entered after a time, both were slightly flushed. Mark rose and shook his dad's hand.

"Dad, this is Doris Tims. Doris, my dad Glen Black Feather," said Mark.

"I'm pleased to meet you, Mr. Black Feather," said Doris, holding out her hand to shake.

"Call me Glen, please," said Glen. "Welcome to our home. We are glad you are safe with us, and you are welcome to stay as long as you need to." He took Doris's hand and, instead of shaking it, he gave it a squeeze.

"Thank you," said Doris, flushing slightly and glancing at Mark. Mark smiled at her encouragingly and put his arm around her shoulders. Glen smiled at this obvious sign of affection.

While Daisy and Doris put supper on the table, Mark took his dad out to the porch and filled him in on everything happening. When he finished explaining, Glen patted him on his shoulder.

"Do not worry," he said. "We will keep your lady and her family safe," he said.

"Thanks, Dad," said Mark.

Daisy called, and they went inside to eat. They all joined hands and Glen said a prayer of thanks before eating.

"So, Dad, how did things go in the capital?" asked Mark.

Glen sighed. "I think we may have accomplished some of our goals. Time will tell," he said.

"Joey, I hear you have a new sister. After supper, you will have to take me to see her," said Glen.

"Sure, Paw Paw, I want to see her, too," said Joey.

"You haven't seen her yet?" Glen asked.

"No, Sir., said Joey shaking his head.

Glen shook his head. "It's high time you did."

Joey smiled big and went back to eating. Joey thought for a minute and then looked at Orin and Sarah. "It's not far to my house," he said. "We will still be able to play together."

"Of course you will," agreed Mark. "You will still see each other in school, too."

Orin and Sarah looked like they didn't know whether to believe in the assurances. They had been through so much. They were programmed to expect the worst.

After the meal was finished, Glen looked at the sad faces of Orin and Sarah and sighed. "Would you two like two like to go with us to see the new baby?" Both children brightened and nodded their heads.

Doris took Daisy's hand and told her to go with Glen. "Mark and I will clear the table and clean up," she urged.

Daisy smiled and took off her apron. "Thanks," said Daisy, following Glen and the children out to the car. The children were in awe of the baby. They did not remember being this close to a newborn before.

"She's beautiful," said Glen to Willow and Logan.

Logan picked Joey up and held him so he could get a better look.

"You are going to help us look after your sister," said

Logan. "Moon Walking said we were going to have our hands full with her."

"Oh, my," said Daisy. Glen started laughing.

"You have a big family to help," said Glen.

"I know," agreed Logan.

"Moon Walking always manages to get the last say," said Glen.

"Well, she may have the last word, but I have found it pays to listen to her," said Daisy.

Glen put his arm around Daisy's shoulder. "I know, Love, so have I," said Glen.

"We have to go. These children have to get to bed. They have school tomorrow. Joey, thank you for visiting with me," said Daisy.

Joey came over and gave her a hug. "I love visiting with you, Maw Maw," he said.

Everyone said goodnight, and Glen and Daisy headed home with Orin and Sarah.

When they arrived home, Doris and Mark took the children up to bed and left Daisy and Glen outside to enjoy some quiet time together.

"Doris?" asked Sarah.

"What, dear?" Doris asked.

"Are we going to live here now?" asked Sarah.

"I don't know. Do you like living on the reservation?" Doris asked.

"Yes, I do. The boys and girls here are much nicer than the ones at my old school. They used to pick on me and Orin and make fun of us," said Sarah.

"Why didn't you tell me?" asked Doris, visibly upset.

"You had so much to do with work and taking care of us, I didn't want to cause any trouble. Besides, some of the boys and girls said we should be taken away and put in a home. We were afraid to say anything. We thought someone would come and take us away," said Sarah.

"Oh baby," said Doris, hugging Sarah tight, "nobody is going to take you away. I won't let them. Get some sleep. I'll be up in a little while."

She tucked Sarah in and kissed her good night.

When she went out of the room, Mark was waiting. She turned into his arm, shedding the tears she had held back in front of Sarah. Mark held her close and made soothing sounds.

When she could control her tears, she looked up at Mark. "Those children got their information from their parents. It makes me furious they were trying to get Orin and Sarah taken away from me. Those meddling busybodies."

"It's not going to happen. I won't let it happen. I will take care of it. I love you, and I love those kids. We are going to raise them together."

CHAPTER 4

*D*oris and Mark joined his parents in the living room. Daisy noticed Doris had been crying and asked what was wrong. Mark explained about the kids being bullied and how some busybodies were trying to have Orin and Sara taken away from Doris and put in foster care.

"They can't take those children. Can they?" she asked Glen.

"They might," said Glen. "If they can slip in and take them, you would have a very hard time getting then back."

"What can I do?" asked Doris.

"You need to file for custody of them before anything happens. We can make out the papers and have them ready when everything is settled with the trial." He took out a pad and pencil. "Let me get some information, and I will draw up the papers."

Glen looked at Mark. "The CPS might try to keep them from being raised on the reservation," he said. Mark nodded his head.

"Now, last name Tims," said Glen.

"No, their dad was my stepfather. Their last name is Larks," said Doris.

"Larks," repeated Glen. "Alfred Larks?"

"Yes. Did you know him?" asked Doris.

"Yes, he was my cousin on my mother's side. He was half-white. His dad was white." Glen smiled with satisfaction. "This will make things easier. They can't complain about the children being on the reservation if they are part Indian," he explained. Mark and Doris both looked at each other and smiled.

Daisy chuckled. "You are more part of the family than you knew," she said.

"Not as much as she is going to be," replied Mark. Doris looked at Mark and grinned. "I think I may be able to slow the CPS down a bit so we have more time to prepare," said Mark.

He took out his phone and called James. "Hello, Mark," said James. "This is becoming a habit," he laughed.

"I have a problem I thought you might be able to help me with," said Mark.

"You haven't seen any of Derrick's friends, have you?" asked James,

"No, nothing like that, the CPS may be trying to take Orin and Sarah and put them in foster care. Some old biddies in town were pushing for it. I was wondering if you could talk to the Judge and see if he can help," said Mark.

"Sure, I'll talk to him and see if he can help. What are their names?"

"Doris's name is Doris Tims. The children are her half-brother and sister. Their names are Orin and Sarah Larks. Their father was half-Indian and my dad's cousin. I really appreciate anything you can do," said Mark.

"I'll talk to the Judge tomorrow and get back to you. Stay safe," said James as he hung up.

Mark looked at Doris and smiled. "He's going to talk to the Judge tomorrow and call me back."

"Do you think the Judge will help?" asked Doris.

"You could not have a better person on your side," said Glen.

"I have had some dealings with Judge Hawthorn. He is a really stand-up guy," agreed Mark. Mark pulled Doris into his arms and gave her a hug. "Everything is going to be alright," he said.

Doris rested her face on his chest and sighed. She was glad this family was on her side. They were a force to be reckoned with, and they were her family. She smiled.

Mark took Doris's hand and led her out to the porch. He wanted some semi-alone time with her. Once outside, he settled into a rocking chair and pulled her into his lap. Doris lay back in his arms and snuggled close to him. She took a deep breath. She loved the way he smelled. It was a crisp, manly smell. Mark laughed and then kissed her.

When the kiss ended, Doris became serious. "I'm not going to be able to go back to my job at the coffee shop, am I?"

"No," replied Mark. "It's not safe."

Doris sighed. "I have some life insurance money from Mom and Alfred. I was hoping to be able to save it for Orin and Sarah. I used the last of my dad's life insurance to take some college classes. I had to drop out when Mom and Alfred were killed. The job at the coffee shop was all I could find. It will be harder to convince the CPS to let me keep Orin and Sarah if I am not working."

"It will not matter. You are on the reservation now. We have different rules. Since the children are part Indian, we have a better chance of keeping them. Besides, you are going to marry me. I will have our new house built large enough to handle two extra."

"Who says we are going to marry," teased Doris. "I haven't heard a proposal."

"I didn't think you were ready for a proposal, yet. Everything has happened so fast, I wanted to give you time to get to know me. I wanted to make sure you did not think I was another stalker."

Doris put her hand on his face and caressed it slightly. "I could never believe you were a stalker. You are the kindest man I know. I don't know anyone else who would have dropped everything and worked so hard to keep us safe. I love you," whispered Doris. She leaned forward and kissed him.

Mark took over the kiss and deepened it. After a few minutes, he drew back slightly. "Doris Tims, will you do me the honor of being my wife and making us a family?" he asked.

"Oh yes," agreed Doris, joining him in a long and satisfying kiss.

When they came up for air, Doris took his face in her hands and looked into his eyes. "Have I told you what a wonderful man you are? You didn't even know me and you jumped right in and helped me, and then you gathered up my brother and sister and kept us all safe. You didn't stop to ask questions. You just forged ahead and made sure we were safe, even bringing us to your own home. There are not many men who would go out of their way to do anything like this," said Doris.

"From the moment I saw you in the mirror, I knew you were mine to protect, love, and cherish. Your soul spoke to my soul. Whether we knew each other did not matter. Our souls recognized each other. I knew I had to keep you, Sarah and Orin safe. I knew my life would be empty without you," Mark finished with another kiss.

When they relaxed and sat back quietly in each other's

arms, Mark looked down at the woman in his arms. He thanked the Great Spirit for sending her to him. He promised he would protect her with his life.

"What were you studying in college?" he asked.

"I was taking cosmetology classes," answered Doris.

"After everything is straightened out, you can go back and get your degree. The reservation could use a good hair salon. It would keep our ladies from having to go into Rolling Fork to get their hair done," said Mark.

"Do you think so?" asked Doris. "It would be great and I could use some of the insurance money to pay for it."

"No, the insurance money needs to be put into accounts for Sarah and Orin's future. I will cover the cost of your classes," said Mark.

"Can you afford to cover my classes? You have a house to build. I don't want to be a burden," said Doris.

"You could never be a burden. I have plenty of money and I make a good salary." Mark smiled. "Building a house on the reservation is a little different than building a house in town. I will have to buy the building materials and have them ready at the site. The men on the reservation will get together and build the house. The ladies will come and bring food and drinks. It will be like a large picnic. Even the older boys will help by bringing materials to the workers. The older girls will help by taking care of the younger children."

"Wow," said Doris. "That is amazing. I'm going to love living here."

Mark laughed. "I am going to love having you live here with me."

They didn't talk again for a while.

"We need to go in and get some sleep," said Doris. "Orin and Sarah will be up early to get ready for school."

Mark sighed. "I know. I just hate to let you go. My arms will feel so empty without you in them."

Doris smiled. "I know. I hate to break the moment. It's not every day a girl gets engaged."

Mark's arms tightened around her. "It will be even better when we are married, then I will not have to let you go."

"I like the sound of that," agreed Doris.

After a few more minutes of serious kissing, they rose and went inside. The living room was empty. His parents had retired, so they reluctantly said good night and went to their separate rooms.

Orin and Sarah were a little sad the next morning because Joey wasn't there. Daisy reminded them they would see Joey at school, and they perked up. When the bus blew its horn, they grabbed their lunches and hurried out to catch it.

Doris stood watching them hurry to the bus and waved goodbye to them. Since she now knew they were part Indian, she could see it in their appearances. They both had dark hair and eyes and their skin was darker. It was like they had a permanent tan. They were not as dark as the children on the reservation, but they were darker than the children in Rolling Fork.

Mark joined her on the porch with a cup of coffee. She raised her face to receive his kiss. "Mom's got breakfast ready," he said. Doris turned and went inside with him to eat.

They found Daisy and Glen already at the table eating. Glen was glancing at the newspaper while enjoying his coffee. He put the paper down when Doris and Mark sat down.

"Good morning," said Glen. "I am going to start the papers to have permanent custody of Orin and Sarah approved for you and Mark today. It will take a few days to get it finalized," said Glen.

"Thank you," said Doris.

Doris looked at Mark. "Did you tell them we are engaged?" she asked.

"You are, that's wonderful," said Daisy coming over and giving Doris a hug. "Welcome to our family. I am so happy." She wiped her eyes.

"If you are so happy, why are you crying, Mom?" asked Mark as she came to hug him.

"They are happy tears," she declared.

Glen rose from the table and shook Mark's hand and gave Doris a hug. "Welcome, we are very pleased," he said.

There was a knock at the door. Glen went to answer it. When he came back, he had Moon Walking with him. "I came by to wish Mark and Doris congratulations on their engagement," she said.

"Thank you, Moon Walking," said Mark and Doris.

"Would you like some breakfast?" asked Daisy. "I have some pancakes and fresh maple syrup."

"Yes, I believe I will," agreed Moon Walking.

Mark pulled a chair back for her and seated her at the table. Daisy brought her a stack of pancakes and sat the pitcher of syrup close by. Doris brought her a cup of coffee.

They all sat at the table to continue their interrupted breakfast.

"These are good," said Moon Walking after eating a few bites. "They are almost as good as the ones Little Flower makes."

Daisy smiled at the compliment. She knew how much Little Flower meant to Moon Walking. Little Flower, also known as Angelica Steele, was married to Moon Walking's grandson, Dr. Alex Steele.

"Thank you," replied Daisy. "How is your great-granddaughter doing?"

Moon Walking smiled. "She is growing fast. Little Flower

and Running Wolf are going to provide her with a little brother soon."

"Wonderful," said Daisy. "I am happy for you and your family."

"Thank you. Also, thank you for the pancakes." She turned to Glen. "If you are headed to your office, I will ride in with you."

"I was just getting ready to leave. I will be happy to drop you off," said Glen.

While Moon Walking headed for the porch, Glen grabbed his briefcase and kissed Daisy goodbye. "I'll call you in a while," he promised,

Daisy looked at Doris and laughed. "Moon Walking is a large help around the reservation. The information she passes on is a great help. She genuinely cares about the people and she always has our best interest at heart. If we have to put up with a few eccentrics, it's well worth it to us."

"I agree," said Doris. "She has been a great help to us. Her advice has been well appreciated."

"Yes, it has," agreed Mark.

CHAPTER 5

*M*ark received a call from Captain Michaels the next day. He went outside to take the call. He wanted to hear any news before he passed it on to Doris.

"Hello, James, any news for me?" asked Mark.

"Yeah, a couple of things; first, a couple of Derrick's friends broke into the house Doris had been living in. They didn't have time to do much damage, mostly some graffiti on one wall, before a patrol spotted their motorcycles and arrested them. They are now in lock up. Second, I talked to the Judge. He said he was faxing Glen Black Feather and the Indian council. Since the children's father was Glen's cousin, they have complete authority to decide where they live and who with. He said he would notify the CPS they were to close the case as they had no authority in the matter." James paused for a minute. "I think that should solve your problem with the children."

"Yes, it should. Thanks, James," said Mark with a relieved smile.

"Anytime, how are things with you and Doris?" asked James.

"I asked her to marry me and she said yes," said Mark.

"Congratulations. I am happy for both of you. I can't wait to pass the news on to Cindy," said James.

Mark grinned. "Give my best to Cindy. Tell her we will probably have a service on the reservation. Ask her if she feels up to being here."

"How soon are we talking about?" asked James.

"As soon as I can talk her into saying I do," said Mark.

"You are planning on coming back to work on the force, aren't you?" asked James.

"Yes, at least for now. I am going to build us a house on the reservation, but we can live here and I can commute," said Mark.

"Okay, I'll talk to Cindy. Keep me informed of your plans. Good luck to you and Doris."

"Thanks, I will," said Mark.

They hung up, and James dialed Cindy. Mark went inside to talk to Doris.

Glen had already left to go to his office. Daisy had plates of eggs, bacon, and toast sitting on the table for Mark and Doris. Doris had just sat down when Mark entered.

Doris looked at his smile and breathed a sigh of relief. "Everything is alright," she said.

"Yeah," agreed Mark. "They caught two of Derrick's buddies breaking into the house where you had been living. They have been arrested and are in jail."

"Am I going to be charged with damages?" asked Doris.

"No, I had Jamie and Silas turn your key into the landlord, so it's not your responsibility."

"Good," said Doris. She looked at Mark expectantly. "What else is there?" she asked.

"James talked to the Judge. The Judge sent a fax to Dad and the Indian council saying they are responsible for deciding where and with whom Orin and Sarah are going to live with. He sent the CPS in Rolling Fork a message telling them they had no authority in the case."

Doris jumped up and ran around the table and threw her arms around Mark hugging him tight. Daisy looked on with a big smile on her face.

While they were hugging Mark's phone rang again. He pulled back from Doris and looked at it. Seeing the names of the front gate guards on the screen, he answered it. "Hello."

"Mark, this is Lone Wolf at the front gate. We just had a person claiming to be from CPS in Rolling Fork come through and head for the school. I thought you should know."

"Thanks, Lone Wolf, I'll take care of it."

Mark hung up the phone and called his dad. "Dad, did you get the fax from Judge Hawthorne about Orin and Sarah?"

"Yes, I was just looking it over," said Glen.

"I had a call from Lone Wolf at the front gate. He said there is a person from Rolling Fork CPS on the way to the school."

"I'll meet you and Doris at the school," said Glen.

"Okay," said Mark.

He hung up the phone and grabbed Doris's hand. "Dad's going to meet us at the school," said Mark, headed for the front door.

"Wait for me, I'm going, too," said Daisy. Taking off her apron and following them out the door. They piled into Mark's car and headed for the school.

Glen was pulling up in front of the school as they arrived. They all got out of the cars and started inside together. They could hear the raised voices before they reached the office. When they entered the office, everyone stopped talking and looked at them.

Spotted Leopard, the principal at the school, looked at Glen with relief.

"This lady is looking for two children named Larks. I tried to tell her we have no one by the name of Larks registered here but, she doesn't believe me and is threatening legal action," said Spotted Leopard.

Glen turned to the lady from CPS. "You know you have no authority on the reservation." He held up his hand when she started to speak. "You are trespassing. You are supposed to go through the council for any matter concerning anyone on the reservation."

"This is not about people on the reservation," she said. "This is about two non-Indian children being kept here."

"You are wrong," said Glen. "The children are the children of my deceased cousin, so they are part Indian. Your office was informed this morning by Judge Hawthorn. He sent me this fax giving me and the council full authority over the Larks children."

Glen showed her the fax. She took it and read it over. She flushed and handed Glen back the fax. "I'm sorry, this must have come in after I left my office," she said.

"Next time you have a problem with the reservation, go through the proper channels. It will save a lot of confusion," said Glen quietly.

"Yes, I will." She looked around at Spotted Leopard. "I am sorry for the mix-up,"

Spotted Leopard smiled and escorted her out of his office. He turned and looked at Glen. "I am sure glad you came when you did. Moon Walking told me not to keep any record of the children being here, but the CPS lady would not listen."

Glen laughed. "It is okay. I should have known Moon Walking would have everything under control."

Spotted Leopard laughed with him. "I can always depend on her." Glen, Daisy, Doris, and Mark went outside.

"Thank goodness the children were not disturbed," said Doris. "They would have been so scared."

Daisy patted her shoulder. "It's all taken care of now. You can stop worrying."

"Is it all taken care of, Dad?" asked Mark. "Are Doris and I going to be able to raise Orin and Sarah?"

"I'm sure Moon Walking is already talking to the other council members preparing the way for our petition for you and Doris to be granted custody. Of course, it may not be finalized until you are married, but I'm sure it will all be just a formality."

Glen smiled at Mark and Doris, who was held tightly in Mark's arms.

"Don't worry. I have to get back to my office. I will see you all tonight," said Glen. He kissed Daisy and headed for his car.

Daisy and Doris decided they wanted to go shopping before going home, so Mark turned toward town. They went into the grocery store. Mark went with them and pushed the cart. Daisy stopped and said hello to a lot of the women shopping in the store and a few who were working. She stopped and introduced Doris to many of them. She let them all know she was in agreement with Mark's choice of a wife.

Many of the ladies asked when the wedding was going to be. Mark always smiled and said soon. Doris smiled and agreed with him.

They spent a leisurely time in the store. With all three of them putting items into the cart, it was filled quickly. When Mark pushed the cart through the line, he quickly paid for the groceries before Daisy could. He then pushed the filled cart out to his car and deposited them in his trunk.

"I didn't mean for you to pay for the groceries when I suggested shopping," said Daisy.

"I know, Mom," said Mark, putting his arm around her shoulder. "I wanted to. It's the least I can do. You have been taking very good care of us. I just wanted to say thank you."

"You are my son, and Doris and the children are family, no thanks are necessary," said Daisy.

Mark hugged her. "I love you, Mom."

"I love you, too," said Daisy.

Doris had watched them with a smile on her face. "This was her family," she thought. "How did I get so lucky?" she wondered.

When Mark helped her into the car, she rose up and kissed him quickly before ducking into her seat and fastening her seat belt. Mark entered his seat with a smile. He reached over and squeezed Doris's hand before starting the car and heading home.

Mark sat out on the porch and watched the children play after the school bus dropped them off and they changed their clothes and ate a snack. Dawn had dropped her three off while she went grocery shopping so Orin and Sarah had more children to play with.

Sarah came over and sat beside Mark on the porch step. "Are you going to be our brother?" she asked.

"Yes, I am, after Doris and I are married," answered Mark.

Sarah was quiet for a minute, thinking. "Are Orin and me going to live with you and Doris after you are married?" she asked.

Mark reached over and took her small hand in his. He then lifted her and settled her against him in his lap. "Yes, I am going to build a large house here on the reservation so you and Orin will have a home with us and it will be big enough for more children if we are blessed with them." Mark looked down at Sarah. "Will you be okay with living with us on the reservation?"

"Yes." Sarah nodded her head vigorously. She had a big smile on her face. "We love it on the reservation. We have never had so many friends."

"Well, you have nothing to worry about. Doris and I are going to take very good care of you both," said Mark. Sarah turned around and gave him a big hug, then she took off to play with her friends some more.

Doris came out onto the porch and sat down by Mark in the spot formally taken by Sarah. She had overheard part of his conversation with Sarah. She leaned against him and laid her face on his chest.

"Thank you for reassuring her," said Doris.

"I was just telling the truth," said Mark.

"I know. I have tried to explain the situation to both of them, but it means so much more when they hear it from you," explained Doris.

Mark pulled her close and kissed her lightly. "Are we going to get married on the reservation or are you going to make me say I do in a church?" asked Mark.

Doris smiled up at him. "I can see how enthusiastic you are about the church idea," she said.

"If it will make you mine, I'll go the church route, but the reservation will be much more fun and easier," said Mark.

Doris shrugged. "I am fine with the reservation, just as long as it is legal."

"It is even more binding than the church ceremony. There are hardly ever any breakups after the Indian ceremony," said Mark.

"Okay, sign me up for an Indian ceremony," said Doris.

Mark hugged her close and kissed her passionately.

"Don't think you are always going to get your way," said

Doris gazing up at Mark when they came up for air. "I can have some very strong opinions sometimes."

"I am sure you will make your opinions known, and I will always listen carefully," agreed Mark with a serious expression.

Doris laughed, "I love you."

"I love you, too," said Mark. "I can't wait until we are married."

"Me either," agreed Doris.

"When are you going to start on our house?" asked Doris.

"I have already started. I have asked some of my cousins, who aren't doing guard duty, to clear the land and prepare it for building. I asked a friend in town to draw up some plans for us to look at. I gave him an idea of what we need, and when he gets a rough draft drawn up, we can see if we need to make any changes," said Mark.

"Wow, you really are in a hurry," said Doris.

"You better believe I am," agreed Mark. "I will talk to Derrick Bear tomorrow and see when he will be able to perform the ceremony."

"Who is Derrick Bear?" asked Doris.

"He is a manager at the bank in Rolling Fork. He is also an ordained minister and is a registered Justice of the Peace," said Mark.

"It looks like we will be covered on all counts," agreed Doris.

"By all means, talk to Mr. Bear and let me know when we are going to be one," said Doris.

Mark kissed her again.

"Supper is ready," called Daisy. She stuck her head out the door and smiled when she saw Glen's car pull to a stop in front of the house.

The children came running when Glen exited his car. All

of them were giving him hugs, even Orin and Sarah. Glen hugged them all back and laughed delightedly. He then headed for the porch and kissed Daisy hello.

"Alright, everyone come wash up for supper," called Daisy.

"What about us, Maw Maw?" asked one of Dawn's boys. "Mom said she would be back to pick us up."

"If she comes back before you finish eating, she can wait for you to finish," replied Daisy. "Now, scoot."

All of the children hurried inside.

Mark and Doris started in with Glen.

"Did you hear anything else after our meeting at school?" asked Mark.

"No, I talked to a council member to see if they had received the notice from Judge Hawthorne. They had received it," said Glen. "We just have to wait until you are married, then we can settle everything."

"I am going to talk to Derrick Bear tomorrow and see when he can perform the ceremony," said Mark.

"Good," said Glen.

They all went in and took their places around the table. After holding hands and saying a blessing, they started passing food around to everyone.

Daisy smiled as she looked around the table at her happy family.

CHAPTER 6

After the children left for school the next morning, Mark called Derrick Bear and talked to him about performing the ceremony. Derrick told him he would check his schedule and get back to him. He was out of his office at the time.

The friend Mark had asked to draw up the plans for the house called. He had a rough draft done and asked Mark to come check it out. Mark asked Doris to go along to look at the plans. She agreed, and they headed for town. Mark decided to drive by the building site on the way to see what progress had been made.

"Wow, I'm glad they know what they are doing," said Doris. "I can't tell heads or tails about it."

Mark laughed. "It may look confusing now, but it is coming together nicely."

They got out, and Doris stood by the car while Mark went over to talk to the men. While they were talking, Doris studied the building site. She shook her head. It still looked like they were digging a hole in the ground to her.

Everyone turned and looked when they heard the sound

of motors coming cross country. As the sound came closer, they could make out three motorcycles headed for them.

Mark turned and hurried toward Doris. "Get in the car," he yelled.

Doris, quickly, turned and opened the door to scramble inside and shut the door. Mark ran to the driver's side and got in the car. Before he could start the car, the motorcycles were surrounding the car. Two more men came out of nowhere. They were on horseback. They had lassos twirling above their heads. They let the lassos fly, and two of the motorcycle riders were pulled off their motorcycles and to the ground. The men, on the horses, pulled the lassos tight and jumped off their horses. They ran to the men and they used a rope to tie up the men. They looked toward the remaining man on the third motorcycle. He had stopped and was looking at his companions. He raised his hands in the air and didn't say anything.

Mark and Doris got out of the car and approached the group. They were joined by the site workers. Mark gazed at the remaining man standing by his motorcycle. The man shook his head slightly, and Mark looked down at the other two, who were tied up.

Mark grinned at his cousins, Jamie and Silas. "Thanks, guys," he said.

"We were keeping an eye on you and Doris," said Jamie with a grin.

"Yeah," agreed Silas. "We figured it would be easier to chase motorcycles on horses instead of in cars."

"It looks like you were right," agreed Mark with a laugh.

"What should we do with them?" asked Jamie.

"Call security and have someone come out and pick them up," said Mark.

"What about him?" asked Silas motioning to the third man.

"Tie his hands and put him in the back of my car. I'll drop him off. I'm on my way to town," said Mark.

Doris had moved close to Mark, and he put his arm around her reassuringly. "It will be fine," he whispered.

Doris smiled at Jamie and Silas. "Thank you," she said.

Both men smiled and blushed slightly. "We couldn't let anything happen to the bride and groom. It would spoil the party," said Silas with a laugh.

Doris and Mark laughed, and Mark gave her hand an extra squeeze.

"I'll see you guys later," said Mark as he guided Doris to the car. Jamie went along and put the third man in the back seat of the car.

Mark waved as he drove off. He got a couple of miles down the road before he spoke. "You want to tell me what the blazes you are doing with that group, Leon?" asked Mark.

"I am working undercover little brother. Congratulations on your wedding," stated Leon.

"You know Mom has been worried about you. Couldn't you have found a way to let her know you were alive and well?"

"Wait a minute," interrupted Doris. "You know this guy?"

"Yes, this is my older brother, Leon." said Mark. "Does your undercover work include trying to run over young women?" asked Mark.

"I had nothing to do with Derrick trying to go after your lady. I didn't know about it until it was over. I'm glad he is in jail. He is nuts, but with Derrick out of the way, Mario Casios is set to take over the leadership of the gang. He is just playing along with Derrick until he is convicted. Mario is worse and more cold-blooded than Derrick. The Feds want him bad."

"If he is your brother, then Jamie and Silas knew who he was," said Doris.

"Yes, they knew who he was. That is why they asked me what to do with him. They won't say anything before talking to me," said Mark.

"It's a good thing your cousins think fast," Doris told Leon.

"Yes, it is," he agreed.

"I have to turn you over to security or your cover will be blown," said Mark

"The chief already knows I am working for the feds to stop their drug trafficking. He won't blow my cover," said Leon. They stopped in front of their security office and jail.

"It was nice to meet you, Doris. I'm sorry you got caught up in this mess," said Leon.

"It was nice to meet you, too. You be careful out there. Those guys play for keeps," said Doris.

Mark got out and led Leon inside. He told Doris to wait in the car.

"So," said Doris after they were on their way. "How many sisters and brothers do you have?"

Mark smiled. "I have three brothers and two sisters. You've met Dawn. Summer is the youngest. She is away at college. Logan, Marcel, and Leon are my brothers. Logan, Marcel, and Dawn's husband Hank raise horses. Jamie and Silas probably used their horses this morning." Mark smiled at her.

They had stopped in front of an office while he was talking. "Are you ready to look at house plans?" he asked.

"Yes, could you check and make sure there are no motorcycles in sight before we get out?" Doris grinned at him.

"I think we have taken care of them for now," Mark said with a smile. He then leaned over and kissed her before helping her out and guiding her inside.

A young woman came forward to greet them when they entered. "Hi, Little Swan, is Pepi in?" asked Mark.

"Yes, he is waiting for you," she said. Turning to Doris, she smiled.

"It is nice to meet the one who captured Mark Black Feather's attention," she said with a smile.

Doris smiled back. She looked up at Mark and smiled at him. "It certainly has not been boring since we met," she said.

Little Swan laughed and led them to an office door. She knocked, but opened the door without waiting. "Mark and his lady are here," she said.

The man behind the desk rose and came forward to greet them. "Doris, this is my friend Pepi and his wife Little Swan, they are the best at drawing house plans on the reservation," said Mark.

"We are the only ones on the reservation to draw house plans," said Pepi. "We are the best, though."

Doris laughed and shook the hand he was holding out to her. "I'm pleased to meet both of you. I know very little about house plans. I will have to depend on Mark to make sure they are okay."

"You can look. If you don't understand something, I'll explain it. I want both of you to be happy in your new home," said Pepi.

He took them over to his drafting table and unrolled the floor plans.

Mark and Doris looked over the plans. Mark seemed satisfied with what he saw. Doris understood more after she looked over the plans for a while. After she studied the floor plans, she looked at Mark. "It's really big," she said.

"We need room for Orin and Sarah to have their own rooms," said Mark.

"It has three bathrooms," said Doris.

"Yes, one is off our room just for us. The other two will be for guests and the children to share," said Mark.

Doris sighed and looked up at Mark. She studied his face for a moment. "You don't have to build such a large house to start with. I love you. I am not marrying you to move into a large house," said Doris.

Mark put his arms around her and held her close. "I love you, too. This house is going to be standing when we have grandchildren. I want something to make our family comfortable in, a place where they can grow. It is an investment in our future." explained. Mark.

Doris smiled up at him through her tears and leaned forward and kissed him.

"Okay," she said, smiling up at Mark.

Mark turned and smiled at their audience. "It's a go. We love the plans," he said.

"I'll get right on the final plans," agreed Pepi.

"I hope you both will have many happy years in your new home," said Little Swan.

"Thank you," said Doris smiling at both Pepi and Little Swan.

Mark guided her out to the car. They decided to go for something to eat before heading home. Mark stopped in front of a jewelry store.

"I think it is time we put a ring on your finger," said Mark. He raised her hand to his lips and kissed it. "We also have a tradition on the reservation. When a couple is married, they make each other a bracelet. It is exchanged at the ceremony. We can skip the bracelets if you want," said Mark.

"I don't know how to make a bracelet," said Doris.

"Well. I could show you how to weave it, but we are not supposed to show it until the wedding," said Mark. "Mom or Dawn could help you learn how to make it."

"Okay, I'll talk to your mom and see if she can help me," said Doris.

"Good, let's go see about an engagement ring," said Mark. He helped her out of the car and into the jewelry store. It didn't take long for them to find the perfect ring. They also purchased wedding rings to match.

When they left the store, Doris was wearing her engagement ring. She was so enthralled with it she stumbled when her foot came upon an uneven sidewalk. Mark caught her arm to keep her from falling. Doris smiled up at him. "Thanks," she said. "I can't help looking. It is so beautiful.

Mark smiled down at her and kissed her lightly. "I'm glad you like it," he said.

"I don't like it. I love it," said Doris. She threw her arms around him and squeezed tight.

Mark hugged her back and then led her to a nearby café to eat.

They had a leisurely meal, but they were too busy holding hands and gazing into each other's eyes to pay attention to what they were eating. Mark fed Doris bites off of his plate and she, in turn, fed him from hers. They were so engrossed in each other, no one bothered them. They smiled fondly and left them to their lunch.

When they finished lunch and started home, Mark decided to go by his dad's office before going home. He wanted to let him know about Leon.

They stopped at his office and went inside. The front desk was empty as the clerk had gone to lunch. Mark knocked on the door, and when his dad called "yes," he opened the door.

"Hi, Dad, it's me and Doris. Have you got a minute?" asked Mark.

"Sure, come on in," said Glen. "What are you two up to?"

"Did you know Leon was working undercover for the

feds?" asked Mark.

"Yes, I did. How did you find out?" asked Glen

"He was with some motorcyclists when they came after us at the new house site," said Mark.

"Was anyone hurt?" asked Glen.

No, Jamie and Silas roped and hogtied two of them, and I took Leon into the security office. They are all in jail now. I didn't blow Leon's cover. I didn't want to say anything in front of Mom until I talked to you," said Mark.

"I'll talk to your mom tonight. Thank you both for keeping this quiet. It could mean Leon's life," said Glen.

"You know you can depend on us," he looked at Doris and she nodded.

"Absolutely," said Doris.

"Is there anything we can do to help?" asked Mark.

"Anything we do may put Leon in danger," said Glen. "We can only be ready if he asks for help."

"Okay," said Mark. "We are heading home. We will see you tonight."

Glen came around his desk and shook Mark's hand and kissed Doris on the cheek. "Drive carefully and keep your eyes open," cautioned Glen.

"We will," promised Mark.

They headed out for home. Mark reached for Doris's hand and held it while he was driving.

"I am going to call James when I get home and find out when Derrick's trial is going to be. I want to set a date to be married when Little Bear calls. I want to be sure there are no conflicts," said Mark.

"Good, I will be glad when we can put Derrick in the past and concentrate on us," said Doris.

Mark smiled and squeezed her hand.

"Me. too," he said.

CHAPTER 7

When they reached home, Mark stayed outside to make some phone calls and Doris went inside to find Daisy in the kitchen. Daisy noticed Doris's ring at once. She kissed Doris on the cheek and hugged her.

"It's beautiful," said Daisy.

"Thank you," said Doris. "Mark was telling me about a bracelet I can make to exchange at the wedding."

"Yes, like this one," said Daisy holding up her arm and rolling up her sleeve showing the bracelet above the elbow on her arm.

Doris admired the bracelet on Daisy's arm. "It is lovely. Why is the bracelet worn above the elbow?" asked Doris.

"The men started putting it there because so many of them work with their hands, and it could be a danger to them on their wrists," said Daisy.

"It looks hard to make. I don't know if I can make it," said Doris. "It looks complicated."

"Well, this is a man's version. Glen made it for me. The one I made, Glen is wearing," said Daisy.

"I can help you. I have some materials left from when

Dawn made her marriage bracelet. We can look through them and see what design we can come up with. The only thing is, you can not work on it around Mark. He is not allowed to see it until you tie it on his arm," said Daisy.

"Do we have to wear it all of the time?" asked Doris.

"Yes, there is a superstition about the bracelet. It is said if you remove the bracelet, you break the connection between the couple. Even if they stay together after removing the bracelet, they will not feel the love once shared," said Daisy solemnly.

Doris frowned. "If they put it back on, wouldn't it restore the connection?"

"No," said Daisy. "The bracelet is put on during a solemn ceremony and is blessed. If it is returned in another ceremony, it might return the connection. I don't know. I wouldn't want to take a chance."

"Me either," said Doris with a shiver. Mark came in, and Doris turned to him with a smile. "Is there any news?" she asked.

"Yes, Derrick has a trial date in two weeks. The Judge had a hearing for the two caught breaking into the house. He had them signed up for the army. He gave them a choice: five years in prison or the army. They chose the army. They were young. I guess he is hoping they can be helped to a better life," said Mark.

"I like this judge," said Doris.

"He is very fair. I have heard him sign others up for service. He tries to help the young ones all he can. Sometimes it works and sometimes it doesn't. We all can only do our best," said Mark'

Doris came over and hugged him. "I am very proud of you. I know you do a great job for the force in Rolling Fork," she said.

"I had a great teacher and partner. No one could be a better role model for a rookie than James Michaels. I learned a lot about the law and the people from him,' said Mark.

"You were partnered with the captain?" asked Doris.

"He wasn't the captain then," said Mark.

"Cool," said Doris.

"Yes, very cool," said Mark with a smile.

"Your Mom is going to see if she can help me make a bracelet," said Doris.

Mark turned and grinned at his mom. "Thanks, Mom, I guess I had better get started designing a bracelet, too."

"Just remember I am an amateur. Don't expect too much," said Doris.

"I love you and I love you are doing this for me. Whatever you design, I will love because I will know it is made with love," said Mark.

Doris looked at Daisy. "How did he get so sweet?" she asked.

Daisy laughed. "He always was a sweet talker," she said.

"I mean every word of it," declared Mark.

"I know you do," said Doris. "That is what makes it so sweet."

Mark leaned forward and kissed her lightly. "You want to go outside and wait for the school bus?" asked Mark.

"Sure," agreed Doris. She and Mark headed for the porch with Daisy following them.

They sat on the steps with Doris leaning back in Mark's arms. Daisy settled into one of the rocking chairs.

"Do you know how to ride?" asked Mark looking down at Doris.

"No, I've never ridden," said Doris.

"Would you like to learn?" asked Mark.

"Why?" asked Doris.

Daisy laughed. "I remember I asked the same thing when Glen asked me if I wanted to learn to ride."

"Did you learn how?" asked Doris.

"Not then, but later, he eased me into it," said Daisy. "I can ride, but it is not one of my favorite things to do."

Doris looked at Mark. "We have so much going on. We can think about learning to ride later."

"Riding can be fun and relaxing," said Mark.

"Not when you have to have bodyguards along," said Doris.

"You are right," said Mark. "Having another person along is not what I had in mind."

Doris looked at Mark grinning at her and blushed slightly. Daisy chuckled as she rocked.

"Here is the bus," said Daisy, spotting the bus coming down the road.

The bus stopped and Orin and Sarah hurried off the bus and ran toward the porch.

"The teacher put me down for class and gave me some homework," said Orin with a big smile on his face.

"I have homework, too," said Sarah holding up a hand full of papers stapled together.

"Great," said Doris. "Moon Walking must have given the school the all-clear for you two to be official students," said Doris.

"Let's get you two inside and changed so you can have a snack and do your homework," said Doris.

She got up to go inside, and Daisy stood to follow them inside. Mark stayed on the porch, sitting quietly, gazing off into the distance. He was usually working. It was a rare occasion when he could just sit and enjoy the quiet.

～

After supper, Daisy, Doris, and Sarah went into Daisy's sewing room. Daisy rummaged around in the closet and brought out a box of bracelet-making materials. She carried the box over to her cutting table and opened it. Inside were strips of leather dyed different colors.

Daisy took out one of the strips and showed it to Doris and Sarah.

"These strips are used for the base. They are soft and will not irritate your arm. We can get them already colored for different backgrounds, so they do not have to be colored. We have the tiny beads to make the design with and the tiny needle is used to attach the beads to the leather to make the design. There are long thin strips of leather to tie the bracelet to the arm."

Daisy took out a tablet of blank sheets of paper and handed it to Doris.

"You can use this to sketch your ideas, and we can see what will be needed to make your bracelet," said Daisy.

Doris took the tablet and opened it to the first page. She took up the pencil and sat looking at the paper. After thinking about it, she started to draw. She drew the leather strip first. At the top of the strip, she drew a sun. It looked like a ball with little lines coming out around it. She drew it small to fit on the leather strip. Down below the sun, she drew a star. At the bottom of the strip, she drew a crescent moon. She handed the tablet to Daisy.

"Daisy looked at the design and smiled. "This will not be hard to make. A simple design is best. It will work up easier. When you have worked your designs into the bracelet, you can put a row of beads down each side to make it look fancier. You don't have to. It's your design. You can make it as simple or as fancy as you want. I like your design. "

"Now, we pick out the color of your starting strip," said Daisy.

Doris studied the strips and picked out one she liked.

"I like this one," said Doris. "See how it starts out with light blue. It will be perfect for the sun. The color changes to a darker navy blue, which will be good for the star. The bottom is so blue it looks almost black. It will be perfect for the moon."

"It is a good choice," said Daisy. "It will make the bracelet stand out."

"For the sun, these small long beads will do for the rays coming out from the sun." Daisy took six long yellow beads and set them aside. The small round yellow beads will do for the sun and star. The moon can use the darker yellow beads," Daisy sat the packets of yellow beads aside. "The border would look good with a mixture of beads. We can pick them out after we make the design."

Daisy put all of this aside and took out the needles and thread. "This thread is very thin. It is also very strong. It is almost like fishing line. It will last forever. You can not break it. It is weaved in and cut." She pulled out one of the needles and threaded it for Doris and handed it to her.

"Wow," said Doris. "It feels so tiny and light."

"Yes," said Daisy smiling.

Sarah leaned in close to get a better look. She had been an enthralled observer. "It looks so pretty," she said of the design on paper.

"Thanks," said Doris, giving her a hug.

"Will I get to make one when I grow up?" asked Sarah.

"You just might," said Daisy. "If you grow up and fall in love with someone on the reservation."

"That's what I will do," declared Sarah.

Daisy and Doris chuckled at her serious expression. Sarah just looked more determined.

"She just might do it," said Daisy, looking at Sarah.

"She just might," agreed Doris.

"We need to put the ones for your bracelet materials aside and store the rest for tonight," said Daisy. "We need to see if the guys have gotten lonely without us."

They put all the supplies away. Doris had hers set aside. When they were finished, they went down to find Glen, Mark, and Orin watching a ballgame on television. They were very into the game. The ladies went into the kitchen to fix a plate of cookies and some glasses of iced tea.

"I guess they didn't miss us," said Doris.

Daisy laughed. "You put the guys in front of a ballgame and they zone out," she said.

"I bet I can get his attention," said Doris, smiling slightly.

Daisy laughed again. "I bet you can. Love always tops a ballgame." Doris laughed with her.

While Sarah carried the plate of cookies, Daisy and Doris carried the glasses of iced tea. They took them into the living room and sat them on the table in front of the guys.

Doris went around by Mark and sat down close to him. His arm came around her, and he smiled down at her.

"Hi," he said.

Daisy smiled and went over and sat next to Glen. He turned and, putting his arm around her, pulled her close.

Sarah sat in one of the rockers and smiled at Doris and Daisy.

Orin scrambled down onto the floor and continued to watch the ballgame.

Glen looked up at Daisy. "Do we have any chocolate cake left from supper?" he asked.

"Yes, would you like a slice?" asked Daisy.

"I believe I will take a slice," said Glen.

"I will get it for you," said Daisy, rising.

"I will come with you," said Glen, rising with her and keeping his arm around her as they left the room.

Doris looked after them thoughtfully. "He's going to tell her about Leon."

Mark nodded. "I believe so."

"Who's Leon?" asked Orin.

"He is my older brother," said Mark.

"Where is he?" asked Sarah.

"He's working off the reservation," replied Mark.

"Will he back, soon?" Sarah asked.

"I'm not sure. I hope so," responded Mark.

"Me, too," said Doris.

"Have you met Leon?" asked Orin.

"Yes, briefly," replied Doris.

Daisy and Glen came back into the room. Glen had his arm around her, and her eyes were bright. She looked like she was fighting back tears. She looked at Mark and smiled bravely.

"I need you to take me into town tomorrow after the school bus runs," she stated.

"Sure, Mom, anything you need," replied Mark.

Daisy shivered. "I need my family home and safe," she said softly.

Glen hugged her close and whispered in her ear. It was so soft they could not hear what he said. Daisy heard him because she turned her face into his chest and snuggled close.

There was a knock on the door, and Glen turned to open it. He found Logan and Joey outside.

"Hi, everyone, Joey needed to get out away from baby things for a time, so I thought I would bring him over to play with Orin and Sarah for a little while," said Logan.

"You guys want to go out and play with Joey?" asked Doris with a smile.

"Yes," all three children said as they nodded their heads.

"Okay," said Doris. "Scoot." The children hurried outside.

Logan looked closely at Daisy and came over and clasped her hand. "What's wrong? You look like you have been crying."

"I just told her about Leon working for the government," said Glen.

"What!" exclaimed Mark and Daisy at the same time.

"You mean Logan knew, too. This is one poorly kept secret," said Mark.

"I had to tell Logan when I went to the capital. I wanted him to keep an eye on your mom while I was gone," said Glen.

"I haven't told anyone. I didn't even tell Willow. I didn't think she needed the stress with the baby coming," said Logan.

"Has something happened to Leon?" asked Logan.

"He's alright. He is still working undercover. He and two other gang members are guests of reservation security. The other gang members do not know who he is. He goes by the name of Dazzler. They seem to think he has a way with the ladies," chuckled Glen.

"Why are he and the others in lock-up?" asked Logan.

"He was with two others when they started harassing Mark and Doris at their building site. Jamie and Silas roped and hogtied the others, and they are all in jail for now," said Glen.

"Can we do anything to help him?" asked Logan.

"No, if we try to do anything, we will blow his cover. Leon seemed to think the case is coming to a head. So we need to stay out of it," said Glen.

Daisy turned away to hide her emotion. Glen pulled her into his arms to comfort her.

Logan shook his head and looked at Mark. "I hate feeling so helpless," he said.

"I know what you mean. All of the time I was driving Leon to lock-up, I kept thinking of ways to help," said Mark. He shook his head. "There was nothing I could do but take him in."

"Leon understood," said Doris squeezing his hand.

"I know," said Mark. "I will be glad when they take the drug traffickers out of circulation and Leon can come home."

"We all will, Son. We all will," said Glen.

CHAPTER 8

The next morning, they were all at the table eating breakfast. Orin and Sarah were getting ready to catch the school bus. Daisy and Doris were talking quietly. Glen was reading one section of the paper, and Mark was reading the police report section.

There was a knock at the door, and Glen and Mark went to see who it was. When the door was opened, a young woman was there, a very pregnant young woman.

"Can I help you?" asked Glen.

"Is this the Black Feather home?" asked the young woman.

"Yes," answered Glen. "Is there something I can do for you?"

By this time Daisy and Doris had joined them. "For heaven's sake, ask the young lady in and let her sit down," said Daisy.

Glen stood back and motioned for the young lady to enter. "Please, come in," he said.

"Thank you," she said.

She came in and sat in one of the rocking chairs. When she sat down she gave a heavy sigh.

"How close are you?" asked Daisy.

"I should have another month, but I didn't want to wait any longer to try and find you. I wanted to see if you knew how I could get in touch with Leon. He doesn't know about the baby. I haven't seen him in seven months, and I didn't know I was pregnant then." She looked around at the confused faces and shook her head. "Maybe I should start over," she said.

"My name is Glenda Jacobs. I was recruited by the feds out of college. They made me Leon's contact person so he could pass information to them. I was supposed to be his girlfriend as a cover. We fell in love, but when the feds found out I was pregnant, they put me in a desk job and sent someone else out to be Leon's contact. They wouldn't let me have any contact with him. They were afraid I would blow his cover. I went along with their orders for a while, but the closer I came to delivery, the more I wanted to let Leon know, but I didn't know how to find him. He had talked about his family so I thought you might be able to help me find him." Glenda looked around at the stunned faces around her. "Can you help me?" she asked.

Daisy looked at Glen. "Yes, we can," she said. "First, we need to get some food in you and let you stretch out and rest a while."

"I don't want to be any trouble," protested Glenda as Daisy helped her from her chair and led the way to the kitchen.

The bus horn blew, and Doris hurried Orin and Sarah out to catch the bus.

"Don't tell anyone about Glenda," she cautioned.

"We won't," they promised.

Doris waved them off and went back inside to see if she had missed anything.

Daisy had Glenda in the kitchen, and Glen and Mark were in there with them. They were talking quietly. When Doris joined them, she stood next to Mark and he put his arm around her.

"Glenda, I'm Leon's Mom. You may call me Daisy." Daisy pointed at Glen. "This is Leon's Dad. His name is Glen. Standing next to Glen is Leon's brother Mark and his finance Doris."

"I'm pleased to meet all of you," she said. "I'm sorry I had to come out so early, but I wanted to slip away. I am sure the feds are keeping a watch on me to keep me away from Leon, and I did not want to have my baby in one of their cells."

"Don't you worry," said Daisy. "You are not having the baby anywhere but here. We have an excellent midwife on the reservation, and the feds have no authority on the reservation."

Daisy took Glen's arm and led him into the other room.

"Glenn Black Feather, you call the security office and tell them to keep all of their prisoners there until we can get down there and talk to them."

"Yes, Ma'am," said Glen. He gave her a quick kiss and took out his phone. Daisy waited a minute and then turned and went back to the kitchen.

"Mark, there are twin beds in Orin's room, you move in with him, and Glenda will have your room," said Daisy.

"I don't want to put anyone out," said Glenda.

"It is fine," said Mark. "I don't mind at all. Orin is good company."

Mark left to move his things and clean the room for Glenda. Doris followed after him to help.

Daisy sat at the table with Glenda. "Glenda, Leon is on the reservation but he is in lock-up."

Glenda stopped eating and stared at Daisy. "Why?"

"He was with two other gang members when they were harassing Mark and Doris at the place where they are building their house. He had to be arrested along with the others so his cover would not be blown," said Daisy.

"Will I be able to see and talk to him?" asked Glenda.

"I am going in to see him myself this morning. You can come with me. We will try to work it so he will be safe and not blow his cover." Glenda's eyes were bright with unshed tears.

"Do you have any family, Glenda?" asked Daisy.

"Yes, I have my parents and two younger sisters. I went to them for help. As soon as my dad found out I was pregnant, he threw me out. He said I was a tramp and I was a bad influence on my sisters."

"Don't you worry," said Daisy, holding Glenda's hand. "You are safe here and we will make sure no one bothers you."

Mark and Doris came back in after moving Mark's things. "Do you have anything in the car to bring in, Glenda?" asked Mark.

"I just have a small bag of clothes. I couldn't carry much with me with the feds watching," she said.

"If you will give me your key, I will bring it in for you," said Mark.

Glenda took her key from her purse and handed it to Mark. "Thanks," she said.

Glen came back into the kitchen. "I talked to Roy Hawk. He is going to make sure the prisoners stay put. Moon Walking called. She is going to meet us at the jail in two hours. She said she had some arrangements to make first."

"What arrangements?" Daisy asked.

"She didn't say," said Glen.

"Okay," said Daisy. "I'll show Glenda to her room. She can rest for awhile, and then we can go to the jail."

"I'll be alright," said Glenda. "I don't need to rest. I just need to see Leon."

"I know," said Daisy, putting an arm around Glenda and guiding her toward her room. "We can't see Leon for two hours so you may as well rest. I'll come and get you in an hour."

She helped Glenda lay on the bed and pulled a blanket over her. Then she went back down to the kitchen. As soon as she was in the kitchen, she went into Glen's arms. They closed around her securely.

"It will be alright," he said. "It will all work out."

Daisy looked up at Glen. Mark and Doris were sitting at the table.

"How can parents treat their children in such a way?" she asked. "Glenda told me her dad threw her out because she was pregnant," said Daisy.

"I know," said Glen. "I heard the two of you talking. I didn't want to interrupt."

"We heard, too," said Doris.

"Any family on the reservation would help a pregnant woman or even one who was not pregnant. They would do their best to help any person needing help. I can not bear to think of a child being thrown out to fend for themselves." Daisy gave Glen another squeeze and then raised her face and took a deep breath.

"I'm alright. I just needed to vent," she said. "I wonder what Moon Walking is up to."

"I guess we will find out when we meet her at the jail," said Mark.

"There is no telling," said Glen.

"There is never a dull moment," said Doris smiling.

Mark hugged her close. "I bet you will look beautiful when you carry our child," he said, laying his hand on her stomach.

"You hold it right there," said Doris. "There's not going to be a child in there until after we have a ceremony." Doris mock-scowled at him. Daisy and Glen laughed at them. They knew Doris and Mark were trying to lighten the atmosphere.

Glenda managed to fall asleep for a while, even though she did not think she could. Daisy went to wake her up in an hour so she could freshen up before going to town. When they reached the office of reservation security, Moon Walking had not arrived. They went inside and Roy Hawk greeted them.

"I'm sorry you are going through all of this trouble, Daisy," said Roy.

"It's not your fault, Roy. I just wish my family had kept me informed. I am not some hothouse flower who needs to be pampered," said Daisy, glaring at Mark and Glen.

"I didn't know," protested Mark.

Glen just threw his hands up and shrugged. "What is done can not be changed. We love you and wanted to protect you from worry."

Roy turned away to hide his grin. He spotted Glenda behind the group. When Daisy saw Roy looking at Glenda, she motioned Glenda forward.

"Roy, this is Glenda Jacobs. She is carrying Leon's child. She needs to talk to Leon," said Daisy.

"Miss Jacobs," said Roy. "Morris from the feds told me to keep you away from Leon if you showed up here."

Glenda looked faint. Doris took her arm to support her.

Moon Walking came in the door. She had heard Roy's last statement.

"The feds do not run the reservation. They don't even do

a good job of running their own offices. Morris has been keeping this young couple apart, just because he could. He has nothing more to say about it. She is on the reservation now. If he calls again, tell him to go back to his world."

Moon Walking went over to Glenda. "Welcome to the reservation, Glenda. Your son is doing fine. Stop worrying. Leon will soon be free of the feds and the two of you can start to build a life for yourselves and your son."

"Thank you," said Glenda, smiling through her tears.

Moon Walking turned back to Roy. "Now, bring the three prisoners into a room so I can look them over." Roy motioned for his deputy to take the prisoners into a room.

Moon Walking turned to the others, "If you will wait until I take care of the others, I can be sure you can meet with Leon safely." Everyone nodded their agreement and sat to wait until Moon Walking was finished.

The three prisoners were in the room when Moon Walking entered with Roy. She stood and looked them over thoroughly for a few minutes. She did not say anything. One of the prisoners, an older man, sneered at her.

"What do you want?" he asked.

Moon Walking did not say anything to him. She turned to Roy. "Have this man transported to the mine. Turn him over to Soaring Eagle. He is to be there for six months and is to be kept chained and well guarded with no communication until further notice."

Roy nodded to his deputy, who came and took the man heavily chained out to be transported to the mine.

"Let him know his motorcycle is in lock-up and will be returned to him at the end of six months," said Roy.

Moon Walking looked at the other man. He was younger and looked scared. "Do you know anything about horses?" asked Moon Walking.

"No, Ma'am," he said.

"Would you like to learn about them?" she asked.

"I guess so, if it will keep me out of jail," answered the young man honestly.

Moon Walking smiled. "An honest answer, it will indeed keep you out of jail. You must also promise to have no further contact with the gang. Your motorcycle will be kept until we are sure you can be trusted."

"Yes, Ma'am, I promise no more gang. I wanted out anyway, but I was afraid they would kill me before they would let me go."

Moon Walking nodded. "You are right. They will not know what has happened to you. They will think you are dead. So you have to be sure to avoid Rolling Fork until they are taken care of."

Moon Walking nodded to Roy. "Have this young man taken to Logan and Marcel Black Feather. Tell them to keep an eye on him. He is to be trained as their new horse wrangler."

"Thank you, Ma'am. I won't let you down," said the prisoner.

Roy nodded to another deputy, and he came forward and took the young man away.

Moon Walking turned to Leon. Leon grinned at her. "Hello, Moon Walking," he said.

"Leon Black Feather," said Moon Walking. "You have sure stirred things up."

"I did not mean to," he said. "I was trying to do my job."

"The man you are working for is not what he seems. You can not trust him. I have to go. Your future is waiting for you in the front office. Make sure you finish with the feds and leave them behind as soon as you can."

Moon Walking left, leaving Leon confused about what

she was saying. Roy came over and unlocked Leon's handcuffs. He pointed to the front office and let Leon go first. Leon stopped when he saw a room full of people waiting for him. He smiled at Mark and Doris. His gaze met Daisy's and she jumped from her chair and hurried over to hug him. He hugged her tightly, and then he spotted Glenda over her shoulder. Glenda smiled at him slightly. He let go of Daisy and hurried over to Glenda. She was trying to stand but was having a little trouble.

Leon pulled her up into his arms and hugged her tightly. "Morris would not tell me where you were. He just said you had asked to be reassigned," said Leon.

"I did not ask to be reassigned. He reassigned me when he found out about the baby. He would not let me tell you about the baby. I guess he was afraid I would blow your cover. He even has had me followed to be sure I did not try to find you."

Leon's mouth drew into a stern line. "Morris has a lot to answer for. As soon as this case is over, I am done with him."

He put his hand on Glenda's stomach. He felt the baby kick, and his face broke out into a big smile. He looked around at his family and smiled really big. "I'm going to be a dad," he said. They all laughed with him.

The door opened, and Derrick Bear came in. "Hi, everyone, Moon Walking told me to come over to the jail and to bring a marriage license," he said.

"You will marry me, won't you?" asked Leon.

"Yes," said Glenda.

Leon looked at his parents. "Will it be alright for Glenda and the baby to stay with you until I finish up with the feds and can build us a house?" asked Leon.

"Of course it is," answered Daisy and Glen at the same time. Daisy looked up at Glen, and they grinned at each other happily.

Derrick Bear had the papers filled out, and Glenda, Leon, and his parents all signed them. He did a quick civil ceremony and married Glenda and Leon then took the license with him to register in Rolling Fork.

Leon kissed his bride and reluctantly turned to his parents to tell them goodbye. Daisy came over and gave him a big hug.

"You take care of yourself. I'm going to be very angry if you let anything happen to you. Besides, you have a family to think about now."

"I know, Mom. I will be careful. Thanks for taking care of Glenda and the baby for me. I love you," said Leon.

"I love you, too," said Daisy.

Leon went with Roy to slip out the back door so he would not be seen. The deputy had his bike waiting by the back door. He shook Roy's hand and roared away.

His family left through the front door. Daisy and Doris were on either side of Glenda making sure she was alright. Glen and Mark led them to Mark's car where they helped Daisy and Glenda into the back seat and Doris into the front. Glen went on to his car to go to work, and Mark headed for home.

Even though Glenda was weepy, she had a smile on her face. She had seen Leon and they were married. He might even be home in time for the baby to be born.

CHAPTER 9

*L*eon wandered into the abandoned warehouse the gang used as a hangout. He strolled over and poured himself a cup of coffee.

Mario eyed him as he found a seat and drank his coffee.

"Where have you been?" asked Mario.

Leon looked up with feigned puzzlement. "I found a new girl, well, really two girls," said Leon with a grin. There were some chuckles from the other guys.

Slingshot was the closest to him. "How are the rest of us going to get lucky if you scoop up all the girls?" he asked.

Leon shrugged. "There are plenty more out there. You just have to be nice to them."

"Have you seen Bull and Slim?" asked Mario.

"Not for a couple of days. Bull wanted to go after the woman who turned down Derrick. He wanted me to go along. I told him no way. I don't try to hurt a woman just because she tells Derrick 'no.' If one woman says 'no,' forget her. There will be three more who will say 'yes.' I'm not going to hurt or kill a woman for Derrick."

"They haven't been back. I wonder if they got caught. I

He turned and left. He motioned for the agents to be shown out. Don Small Eagle was waiting for them and followed them to the gate.

At the Black Feather house, there was a small celebration, even though Leon was not there. They toasted the bride in tea. She could not drink anything stronger. They made a fuss over her and made her welcome. Logan and Willow came over and brought Camille. After the ladies had made a fuss over Camille, Willow had Logan bring in some maternity clothes. Since she and Glenda were about the same size and Glenda had not been able to bring many clothes with her, Willow was sure Glenda could use them.

Glenda got weepy again when she received the clothes. "Thank you all for being so nice to me," she said.

"You are family. We want you to be happy here with us," said Daisy.

"I have never been treated so nice in my life," said Glenda.

"Well, get used to it," said Willow. "The Black Feather family knows no other way." Mark took the bag of clothes up to Glenda's room.

They were all sitting around the table talking when Dawn came in. She had a bag of baby clothes with her. "Hi, Glenda," she said, going over and giving Glenda a hug. "I dug up some baby clothes. I thought you could use them. I know we will all be buying more, but take my word for it. You can never have too many baby clothes."

Glenda flushed slightly. "Thank you. I don't have many baby clothes. Most of them I had to leave behind in my apartment."

"Don't worry," said Daisy. "Doris and Mark can go shopping tomorrow and stock up on diapers and other essentials."

"Sure," said Doris. "I love shopping. It will be good practice for when we start our family." Mark hugged her close to his side and kissed her.

They heard the bus stop out front. Orin, Sarah, and Dawn's three children came into the house and straight to the kitchen.

"Well, hello," said Daisy.

"Hello, Maw Maw," said Dawn's children as they hurried over to give Daisy a hug. "Mom left a note on the mailbox for us to come on over here."

"Orin, Sarah, change your clothes so you can eat a snack and do your homework," said Doris.

Orin and Sarah hurried away to change their clothes.

"Oh, Orin," called Mark after them. Orin turned around and looked back.

"You and I are going to be sharing a room. Glenda has my room," said Mark.

"Cool," said Orin with a smile. He turned and hurried to change clothes.

Mark looked at Glenda and smiled. "See, I told you Orin would not mind sharing." Glenda smiled back at him and Doris who was close by his side.

"Oh, you have your ring," exclaimed Dawn as she spotted Doris's ring. She hurried over to get a closer look. Doris held up her hand for Dawn to get a better look. "It's beautiful," she said.

"Thank you," said Doris.

"Have you set a date?" asked Dawn.

"We are waiting on Little Bear to get back to us," said Mark. He smiled at Doris. "Maybe we ought to have Moon Walking take care of it for us,"

"Moon Walking has done enough for our family," said Daisy.

"I know, Mom, I was just kidding," said Mark.

Glen chuckled. "It seems whenever there is a need on the reservation Moon Walking is there ahead of everyone else. If she has done nothing about your wedding, then she feels everything is progressing as it is supposed to."

"You are right, Dad. No word from Moon Walking means everything is going to be as it should. We will just have to be patient," said Mark.

He gave Doris another squeeze, and she smiled up at him and raised her face for a kiss. Mark was happy to oblige her.

Marcel and Hank joined the crowd. They brought Stanley with them.

"Everyone this is Stanley White," said Marcel after going over and giving Daisy a hug and a kiss on the cheek. "Moon Walking sent him over to be taught to be a horse wrangler."

"Stanley, this is the Black Feather family. I'm sure you will get to know all of us over time, but the most important one to meet is this one." He led Stanley over to Daisy. "This is my mom, Daisy Black Feather. She has us all in the palm of her hand." He hugged Daisy again as everyone laughed.

"It's nice to meet you, Ma'am," said Stanley.

Daisy pulled away from Marcel and looked at Stanley. "We are glad you are here with us, Stanley," said Daisy.

Daisy turned to the children. They had finished their snacks and were sitting back, listening to the adults. "Alright, children, if you have finished eating, take your plates to the sink and go into the living room and do your homework."

"Yes, Maw Maw," said Dawn's children as they all went to do as Daisy directed.

Doris smiled as she saw Orin and Sarah follow the others into the living room.

"Where will Stanley be staying?" asked Glen.

"He's going to be bunking at my place with Buck," said Marcel.

"How is old Buck?' asked Glen.

"He is as strong as a horse and just as stubborn," said Marcel. "I tried to get him to see the doctor about his stiff fingers. He informed me, his fingers have been getting stiff for years. He said it just means it's going to rain. He said there was nothing the doctor could do about the rain," said Marcel.

Everyone laughed. "He could be right," said Glen.

Daisy looked at Glen suspiciously. "Have you been having pain in your knee again?" asked Daisy.

"My knee is fine," declared Glen. He went over and pulled Daisy into a hug. "I promised to let you know if I had any more trouble," said Glen.

Daisy hugged him back. She looked at Glenda and saw she was looking tired. "It's time for you to rest," said Daisy. Glenda tried to protest, but Daisy helped her up and Daisy and Doris helped her to her room. Dawn had included a nice flannel gown in her bag of clothes. Doris got it out while Daisy helped Glenda out of her dress.

"I have asked the midwife to come by tomorrow and check on you," said Daisy.

"Thank you," said Glenda. She was almost asleep by the time Daisy and Doris left the room.

CHAPTER 10

*T*he next day the midwife came by and pronounced Glenda in fine shape. She told her to relax and not stress the baby out. Glenda promised to try.

"It should be easier to relax since I have told Leon about the baby," Glenda told Daisy.

Daisy smiled at her. "We will all relax when Leon is home and done with the feds," she said.

"Yes," agreed Glenda.

"Where is Doris?" asked Glenda. Mark had gone to check on their building site. Jamie had gone with Mark, and Silas had stayed to keep an eye on the women.

"Doris is working on her marriage bracelet. She wanted to work on it while Mark is gone. He is not supposed to see it until the marriage ceremony," said Daisy.

"What is a marriage bracelet?" asked Glenda.

"It is an Indian custom. It is worn on the upper arm and is exchanged at the wedding ceremony. Mark is making one for Doris, also," said Daisy.

"Oh, I guess Leon and I will have to skip the bracelet," said Glenda.

"I don't know. I will ask Moon Walking about it," said Daisy.

"If you want to come into the sewing room, I have some nice flannel material. We can make the baby some blankets," said Daisy.

"I would like that," said Glenda struggling out of her chair.

"One good thing about my sewing room," said Daisy. "It has a nice comfortable rocking chair."

"Lead me to it," laughed Glenda.

Mark walked around the building site. Jamie stood to one side and watched the area around them.

Mark was pleased with the progress the men had made. It was almost ready to start building on. He had made some lists of material he would need to build the house. Maybe it was time to start ordering the building materials. When he had it all at the building site, they could get everyone together and build the house. First, he needed a plumber to make sure the pipes were in the right places.

Mark went over to Jamie. "Isn't one of your cousins on your mother's side a plumber?" he asked.

"Yes, Jerry does plumbing work on the reservation," agreed Jamie.

"Do you suppose he would look over my plans and tell me what I need for the house?" asked Mark.

"I don't know how busy he is, but I will ask him," agreed Jamie.

"Thanks," said Mark.

Mark took out a tablet and started adding to the lists of building materials he would need for the house. Jamie would glance at his list as he wandered around. He would sometimes make suggestions to add to the list. Then he would move on and keep an eye on the surroundings.

When Jamie stopped beside him again, Mark closed his notebook with a sigh.

"I'll get Logan to look it over this evening and see if he has any suggestions," said Mark.

"Good," said Jamie. "It hasn't been too long since he built a house for him and Willow. He should be a big help."

"Yeah," said Mark with a grin. "I was just thinking the same thing."

"Are you headed for home now?" asked Jamie.

"I am going to swing by town first. Pepi called. He has my house plans ready, and I need to pick them up so I can show them to Logan tonight," said Mark.

Jamie climbed into the front passenger seat of Mark's car and they headed for town.

"Hi, Pepi," said Jamie as they entered and found Pepi standing by Little Swan's desk talking to her.

"Hi, Little Swan," said Jamie.

"Hi, Jamie," said Little Swan. "When are you going to settle down and let us design you a house?" asked Little Swan.

"As soon as my true love finds me," said Jamie with a laugh.

"You are tempting fate," said Little Swan. "You had better watch out." Jamie looked around, nervously, like he expected a girl to pop up and claim him. Little Swan laughed and Pepi and Mark joined in.

"You have my house plans finished?" asked Mark.

"Yes, they are right here." Pepi reached into the pile of rolls on the desk and selected the one with Mark's name on it and handed it to Mark.

"How much do I owe you?" asked Mark taking out his checkbook.

"There is no charge. They are a wedding present from Little Swan and me," said Pepi.

"You don't have to do this," said Mark.

"Yes, I do. You are my friend and you are the one who helped me open this office and start my business. Without your help, we would still be struggling and trying to run the business out of our living room. This is the least I can do to show you how much you and your family mean to us both."

Little Swan stood and went to Mark's side. "We will not take 'no' for an answer. Enjoy your new home. Tell Doris it was drawn with love, and we hope you both will enjoy it for many years."

"Thank you both," said Mark giving first Little Swan and then Pepi a hug.

"Come out to visit soon. You can meet Leon's new wife and Logan and Willow's new daughter. I'll get Mom to set everything up," said Mark.

"We will visit soon," agreed Little Swan.

They all said goodbye, and Mark and Jamie left to go home. Jamie didn't say anything but Mark noticed him looking over at him often. "What is it?" he asked.

"I didn't know you helped Pepi and Little Swan start their business," said Jamie.

"I did not see any reason to spread it around. I did not want to cause them any embarrassment. I would appreciate it if you would keep it to yourself," said Mark'

"I won't tell anyone," said Jamie.

"Thanks," said Mark.

The rest of the drive home was accomplished in comfortable silence. When they arrived home, they found Daisy and Doris in the kitchen planning the evening meal.

"Where is Glenda?" asked Mark.

"She is taking a nap," said Daisy. "The midwife said she needed plenty of rest. She has been under a lot of stress for a while now. It will be good for her and the baby to relax and rebuild their energy."

Mark turned to Doris and kissed her lightly. "I picked up the finished plans for our house," he said. "I told Pepi and Little Swan we would have them over to supper, soon, so they can meet Glenda and Camille. Is it okay with you, Mom?"

"It's a great idea. I'll get with Little Swan and arrange something," said Daisy.

"After supper, I want t get with Logan and go over the plans. I thought he could help me order the materials I will need," Mark said to Doris.

"I would love to spend some time with Willow and Camille. Orin and Sarah will love playing with Joey," said Doris.

"Why don't we ask them over here for supper?" asked Daisy. "I want to play with my new granddaughter, also," said Daisy.

"Why not call Willow and see if she feels up to visiting?" asked Mark.

Daisy smiled and picked up her phone to call Willow. "Hello, Willow. Mark wants to have Logan look over house plans with him tonight. I was wondering if you all would like to come to supper?" asked Daisy.

"Sure, we would love to," said Willow. "I can leave Camille at home with my sister."

"Oh," said Daisy in a disappointed voice.

Willow burst out laughing. "I was just teasing, Mom. We will all be there."

"Good," said Daisy, perking right up. Daisy hung up the phone and turned to face Mark and Doris. "They are coming," she said.

"What was the pause about?" asked Mark.

"It was nothing," said Daisy. "Willow said they might

leave Camille with her sister to babysit. She was just teasing me. They are bringing her." Mark and Doris burst out laughing. Daisy smiled sheepishly. "I can't help it. I love being with my grandchildren," she said.

Doris went over and hugged her. "Of course you do," she said.

Mark went to the living room and unrolled the house plans and started studying them.

Daisy and Doris stayed in the kitchen and got a head start on preparing supper for a large group. When they had fixed everything they could fix ahead of time, Daisy went to her sewing room to work on some baby clothes and blankets.

Doris wandered into the living room and sidled up close to Mark. Doris looked at the plans. She still couldn't understand them. She leaned against Mark and watched as he absorbed the plans.

Mark looked down at her and smiled. "I know it doesn't look like it right now, but it will be a nice home when we get finished," he said.

"I believe you," said Doris.

She leaned up and kissed his cheek. "I think I will go and check on Glenda. I may work in my room for a while." Doris rose, smiled at Mark, and went upstairs.

Doris opened the door of Glenda's room quietly and peeped inside. Glenda was fast asleep. She closed the door softly and went to the room she shared with Sarah. When she went inside, she closed the door and pulled the box of bracelet makings out from under the bed. She took it over to a table by the window. The light was better there. She unrolled the work she had already finished and started where she had stopped. She had finished the sun and was working on the star. It was coming along nicely. Doris was surprised at how well the bracelet was coming along.

Doris worked on the bracelet until she finished the star. She looked at the clock and saw it was almost time for the school bus. Doris rolled the work she had done and put it back under the bed.

Doris went by Glenda's room again to check on her. This time Glenda was up and she greeted Doris with a smile.

"I think it will be good for me to go down and move around for awhile," said Glenda. "If I stay up here any longer, I won't be able to sleep tonight."

Doris held her arm as she went downstairs. They went on out to the front porch. After helping Glenda to a rocking chair, Doris sat in another rocking chair.

"It feels good to be out in the fresh air," said Glenda.

"Yes, it does. It's beautiful out here," said Doris. "I hope Mark is building us a big porch we can sit out on and enjoy the cool breezes."

"I have no idea what Leon has planned for us," said Glenda. "As long as he comes home safely, I don't care where we live."

"Well, you have one reason to hope everything will be alright," said Doris. Glenda looked at her inquiringly. "Moon Walking seemed to think everything was going to be alright. From what I have heard, Moon Walking always knows. If she is not worried, you don't have to worry."

Glenda smiled and looked off into the distance. "I love this place," she said.

"So do I," agreed Doris. They sat contentedly rocking as they waited for the school bus.

They had been sitting there a while when Mark came out to join them. He scooped Doris up and sat down in her chair with her in his lap. Doris lay back against him and snuggled close. Mark tightened his arms around her.

Glenda smiled at them. "Leon told me you were on the police force in Rolling Fork," said Glenda.

"Yes, I am," said Mark. "I am on a leave of absence until I am sure Doris is safe."

"I wondered why there was so much security around. Who is threatening Doris?" she asked.

"A man named Derrick Bolin. He is a gang member. He was trying to kill Doris because she didn't want him. He is in jail awaiting trial. We just have to watch out for members of the gang. It is the gang Leon is undercover with," said Mark.

Glenda shook her head. "Maybe it will all be over soon."

"I hope so," said Doris.

They sat quietly talking for awhile. Then Daisy came out to join them. "You all look like you are having a relaxing time," said Daisy.

"We are," agreed Mark. "Would you like for me to bring another rocker out for you?"

"No, I'll just sit on the bench," said Daisy. She settled on the bench and leaned back against the wall. "I finished a blanket for the baby. I put it in your room," Daisy told Glenda.

"Thank you. I was going to help you," said Glenda.

"You needed the rest. You have been under so much stress. You just relax. You will feel better in a few days," said Daisy.

Jamie and Silas came around the house from different directions. They both stopped in front of the porch and grinned up at everyone. "I talked to my cousin about the plumbing in your house," said Jamie. "He said he would look over the plans tomorrow and see what needs to be done."

"Thanks for asking him," said Mark.

"Sure," said Jamie with a shrug.

Silas looked at Doris. "Is it true you saw Mark in the magic mirror?" asked Silas.

"Yes, it is," said Doris, grinning at Silas and then smiling up at Mark.

"I've heard the girls on the reservation talking about the magic mirror. They were all excited about it. I thought they were just dreaming," said Silas.

"It really works. I didn't really believe it either until I saw for myself," said Doris.

Silas and Jamie turned and looked toward the road as the school bus came to a stop for Orin and Sarah to get off.

The bus driver waved at them as he continued on his way. Orin and Sarah hurried to the porch to greet everyone. Doris and Daisy stood to go inside and make sure they changed and did their homework. Doris stopped and helped Glenda up so she could go inside with them.

CHAPTER 11

he guys were all gathered in the living room studying the house plans. Mark had waited until after supper to bring out his plans. The ladies were in the dining room. While Doris and Willow cleaned the table, Daisy sat at the table and held Camille. Glenda sat close to her, watching. Glenda rubbed her stomach. She looked at Camille with longing.

Daisy glanced at her. "It won't be long. You will be able to hold your son," she said.

"I am looking forward to it," agreed Glenda. "I'm a little scared. I have never had much to do with babies."

"We all had to learn by doing," said Willow. "You have all of us for back up."

Glenda smiled. "I am so lucky. Leon has an amazing family."

Daisy looked over and grinned. "You are a very welcome addition to Leon's family."

"Thank you," said Glenda.

Doris came over with a cloth to wipe off the table. She saw

Marcel outside the door of the dining room. "Now, all we have to do is find Marcel a wife," she said loudly.

Marcel burst into the room. "No, you don't. I can find my own wife when I get ready for one," stated Marcel firmly. All the ladies burst out laughing.

"I was just teasing, Marcel," said Doris. Marcel looked at them sheepishly, before turning and disappearing back into the living room. "I hope I did not hurt his feelings," said Doris.

"He will be fine," said Daisy. "It won't hurt him to lighten up a bit. He is too serious sometimes." Doris shrugged her shoulders, but she glanced worriedly at the door to the living room.

In the living room, Logan was making suggestions for more material needed for the house.

"Before you start on the house, you need to get Laughing Elk to pour concrete for the basement in the house. This is Kansas. Everyone should have a storm shelter. After he does the concrete, Jamie's cousin can do the plumbing. Then you will be ready for a house raising. Everything has to be prepared first," said Logan.

Mark sighed. "This is going to take longer than I thought," he said.

Doris came into the room in time to hear Mark's last statement. She went over to stand next to him. Mark put his arm around her and pulled her close.

"We have plenty of time. We don't have to wait for the house to be built to be married. It will be a joy to move into this beautiful house whenever it is ready for us. I'm sure Moon Walking would tell you, 'Everything happens in its own time.' Just be thankful we have each other." Doris raised her face and lightly kissed his cheek.

"How did you get so smart?" asked Mark.

"I guess I have been around you guys so long, you are rubbing off on me," laughed Doris.

"I can hear Moon Walking saying that," said Willow.

"Yes," everyone agreed.

The children came in from outside where Silas had been keeping an eye on them. "We are thirsty," said Joey. "Can we get something to drink?"

"Sure," said Daisy. She handed Camille over to her mother and she took the children to the kitchen to get a glass of water. They all drank thirstily and hurried back out to play.

Glen had joined Mark and Logan looking at the house plans. "Are you going to have enough money to build this house?" asked Glen.

"Sure, I have been saving my checks from the mine for years. It has been sitting in the bank building up," said Mark.

"What mine?" asked Doris.

"It is a mine of semi-precious stones. The reservation owns the mine, but it is on our property, so we get a check from the mining company every six months. The money is divided seven ways. My parents get one share and I and each of my brothers and sisters get a share," explained Mark.

"How can there be so much money in semi-precious stones?" asked Doris.

"They are sold to jewelers all over the country. They make them into costume jewelry. It is a thriving business," explained Glen.

"Where is it?" asked Glenda.

"It is at the northern edge of our property," said Glen.

"The reservation built a road around the edge of our property for the mine to use. They are not allowed to come across our property. It could disturb the horses to have heavy equipment around. We would also have to worry about them leaving gates open and letting our horses out," said Logan.

"Will we be able to ride out and see where it is someday, after I learn to ride?" asked Doris with a laugh.

"Sure, I don't see why not," agreed Mark with a kiss.

"Can you ride?" Doris asked Glenda. "When you are not pregnant,"

Glenda laughed. "No, maybe you and I can learn together, if you don't mind waiting to learn."

"I don't mind at all," assured Doris seriously. Everyone smiled at her answer.

"I think we have studied these enough for tonight," said Mark as he rolled the plans up and put them in their container.

He took Doris's hand and led her over to a rocking chair and, sitting down, pulled her down into his lap. Doris snuggled into his arms and laid her face on his chest and gave a sigh of satisfaction.

Everyone smiled fondly at them.

"I think it's time we headed home," said Logan. "We have to get up early in the morning."

He went over and took Camille from Willow and helped her to stand. He placed a quick kiss on her lips before helping her gather the baby things she had brought with her.

"Thanks for coming over to help me figure out the supplies I needed," said Mark. He and Doris rose to accompany Logan and Willow outside.

"I enjoyed it," said Logan. "Thanks for supper, Mom."

"I was well rewarded," said Daisy gazing at Camille. Everyone smiled.

When the children saw the adults come outside, they came running. Joey told Orin and Sarah goodbye and climbed into his seat. Everyone stood on the porch and waved them off.

"Silas and I are going to have a final look around and then

go get some rest while Don and Tim keep an eye on things. Silas and I will be back in a few hours," said Jamie

"Thanks," said Mark. "We'll be fine. You two need a good night's sleep."

The family all turned and went inside. Glenda was still sitting in her chair in the living room. She smiled as everyone came back inside.

"We didn't mean to leave you in here by yourself," said Daisy.

"I was okay," said Glenda. "I just did not feel like getting up and down again. I thought I would just wait until bedtime or until I needed the bathroom." She laughed.

Daisy laughed, too. "I know how that goes," she agreed.

Doris went with Sarah to see to her bath and help her to get ready for bed. Mark went to help Orin. When both children were tucked up in bed for the night, Mark and Doris met in the hallway. Mark pulled her close and kissed her.

When he pulled back and looked down into her eyes, she smiled up at him. He leaned in for another kiss. When she had to pull away to breathe, Doris hugged him close.

"Your parents and Glenda will be up here soon," said Doris.

"I know," sighed Mark. "I just want you so much. It's hard to wait."

"I know. I want you, too. I love being in your arms. The wedding is only a week away," said Doris. "We will finish with Derrick's trial in a few days. Then we can concentrate on us and our life together."

While she spoke, Mark was raining small kisses over her face and neck.

"I hear someone coming," said Doris.

"Let's go out on the porch for awhile," said Mark. "At least out there, I can hold you in my arms. We can give my parents and Glenda time to get settled for the night."

"Okay," agreed Doris. She held tightly to Mark's hand as they went downstairs. They passed Daisy helping Glenda upstairs. Glen was following along behind them.'

"Good night," said Mark and Doris.

"Doris and I are going to sit on the porch for awhile," said Mark. "I'll lock up when we come in." Glen smiled and nodded as he followed Daisy and Glenda on up the stairs.

Mark unlocked the door and led Doris out onto the porch. He waved to Don and led Doris over to a rocking chair. He sat down and pulled Doris down into his lap. Doris lay back as Mark's arm s closed around her tightly.

"I love being here in your arms," said Doris.

"I love having you here in my arms," whispered Mark. He rested his chin on Doris's head and stared up at the stars. He felt when Doris relaxed into sleep. He smiled and held her tighter.

"Thank you, Great Spirit, for bringing this amazing woman into my life to complete me," he whispered softly.

Doris smiled. She had been on the verge of sleep when she heard Mark's whispered words. She hugged them close to her heart and thought a similar prayer to herself.

After awhile Mark roused himself and carried Doris inside and settled them both on the sofa with her still held close in his arms.

CHAPTER 12

Mario Casios entered the warehouse where the gang members were lounging around. Some were sleeping on sleeping bags; some were watching a television they had rigged up by running a cable line to a nearby office building. Leon was on an old sofa. It had been found by some of the guys and dragged in along with several other chairs and a few tables. He was talking on his phone to his contact. She was another agent and was pretending to be one of his girlfriends.

"Get off the phone, Leon. We have to move out," said Mario.

"Sorry, Sweets, I have to go. I'll talk to you later. Yeah, buy a big box." Leon smiled as he hung up.

"A big box of what?" asked Slingshot.

"What?" asked Leon, pretending confusion. "Oh, condoms, we used all we had and she is going to buy more," he said with a grin.

"You make your ladies buy condoms for you," asked Slingshot as several of the guys snickered.

Leon shrugged. "She offered." Slingshot just shook his head.

"What's her name?" asked Mario. "I only hear you call her Sweets?"

Leon pulled out his phone. "I think her name was Gigi," he said. He looked at his phone for calls received. "Yeah, Gigi," he confirmed.

"You don't know who you were talking to?" asked Mario.

"That's why I call them all Sweets. I won't accidentally call one by another one's name. They get all upset when I do it. So this way we are all happier," explained Leon.

Several of the guys burst out laughing. Even Mario had a smile twitching the corner of his mouth. He just shook his head. Leon went on as if it was nothing unusual.

"Alright, guys, we are moving out. We will be on the road for a few days. So bring your tents and sleeping bags. We may want to camp out on the way," said Mario.

"Where we going?" asked Slingshot.

"We are going to make a run. You don't need to know where. Just get ready to go," said Mario.

"Sure, Boss, you want me to wake up everyone?" asked Slingshot.

"Yeah, tell them they got thirty minutes and then we are moving out. If they aren't ready, we go without them," said Mario.

Leon rolled up his sleeping bag silently. He already had his clothes and other essentials packed in his storage on his bike. He never unpacked his bike except to use something. After using anything, he always made sure it was returned to his supplies on his bike.

The gang members woke up quickly and hurried to prepare for departure. Most of them were glad to be getting out. They were tired of waiting around for something to happen.

In Morris' office, in the feds building, Diane hung up the phone and turned to Morris. "Leon said they are getting ready to make a run. He said it was going to be big. It's supposed to take several days."

Morris picked up his phone to alert his agents. "The gang is on the move. Let them do a pick-up, and we can get them and the drugs when they are on their way home. We need to know the route they are taking."

Morris hung up his phone and rubbed his hands together with satisfaction. "Finally, we can catch them in the act and clean up," he said.

Diane frowned and looked hard at Morris. "He had been acting weird about Leon. She wondered why Morris was so determined to keep Leon and Glenda apart. It did not make any sense. She shook her head, and turning, she left Morris's office.

In a building near the gang's hangout, an agent was watching through binoculars. He watched the motorcycles head down the road. It would be hard to miss the noise of a dozen motor-cycles passing by. He watched until they were out of sight, then he called another agent in a building a few miles down the road.

"They are headed your way. It looks like they are headed toward Mexico." He hung up his phone and hurried to his car. He was going to follow along behind the gang, at a distance.

He didn't want to take a chance on being spotted and alerting the gang to his presence. They had been trying for a long time to bring the gang in. Now was the chance to catch then in the act and get enough evidence to put them away for a long time.

He stopped at the building where the other agent was long enough to pick him up and then continued to follow behind the gang.

"Did you alert the agents up ahead?" the agent asked when he joined him.

"Yeah, there is a spotter every twenty miles. When they pass the last spotter, he will call ahead and have some more agents watch for them. If they turn a different way, we won't have far to backtrack to see where they turned. Morris has had this system set up for months. He is determined to get them this time."

The agents continued following. They listened to the reports of the agents ahead and knew they were on the right track. They made a brief stop at a fast food place to pick up some coffee then continued their pursuit.

The gang continued their journey. They had seen no sign of pursuit and were not worried about being followed. After all, they had not done anything wrong, so far. They were just taking a little road trip. It might scare the people to see so many motorcycles at one time, but everyone soon relaxed when the riders passed on through. Law enforcement might wonder where they were headed, but for the most, they were just glad the motorcyclists kept on going and did not stay in their towns.

After several hours of travel, Mario turned into a state park. He led the gang deeper into the woods away from the road. He stopped in a clearing and turned off his bike. When the other motorcycles were quiet, Mario looked around.

"We'll set up camp here. Sling Shot, you and Dazzler take orders for food and go back to the town we passed a few miles back and pick up some food from a fast food place. I don't want to draw attention to us by having so many bikes stop at one time."

He handed them some money, and everyone shouted out their orders at once. Leon raised a hand.

"One at a time, I can't remember all of this. Sling Shot, you write these down."

They took the orders and headed back the way they had come. They stopped at the first fast food place they came to, and Sling Shot ordered from the list he had written.

As Leon looked around, he spotted the two agents sitting at a table eating. They were looking his way and quickly looked back at their food. Leon turned back to help Sling Shot with their food. They took it all out and stored it in their saddlebags. Then they headed out under the watchful eyes of the feds.

Leon was satisfied to know his message had been received, and the feds were alerted to the gang's activities.

They quickly handed the food out to the hungry gang members when they returned to the campground.

The gang had set up their tents and unrolled sleeping bags, and after eating, they were ready to stretch out in sleeping bags to rest before continuing the trip.

The feds followed Leon and Sling Shot. When they saw them turn into the park, they waited to see if they would come back. When there was no sign of their return, the agents turned into a campsite close to the road and made ready to spend the night in their car. They would take turns sleeping and keeping watch. If the gang noticed them when they left in the morning, they would think it was just someone else camping in the park.

Leon settled down in his sleeping bag. He thought about Glenda and smiled. Soon, he thought, I will hold you and our son in my arms again. This job could not be over soon enough for him. He would be glad to see the last of the feds and return to the reservation and his love.

Glenda was thinking about Leon, also. "Soon my love, soon," she whispered. She then slept with a smile on her face.

The gang was roused early by Mario. One of the gang members had woken earlier and had made a large pot of coffee. The others rushed to get their cups filled before leaving. They did not notice the car parked in the first campsite. They left the park and headed south.

The agents saw the gang members leave the park. They were still headed south. One of the agents called ahead and alerted the agents ahead to the movement of the gang.

"They are still headed south," he said. "Spread the word." The agents continued to follow.

"The first town we come to, with an open café, I want to stop and get some coffee," said the other agent.

"I hear you," agreed his partner.

The gang had gone through drive-through windows two at a time and bought coffee and breakfast sandwiches. They stopped outside of town and quickly ate and drank their coffee before heading south again.

The gang members were unaware they were being tracked by agents all along the way.

It was late afternoon when Mario turned into another state park and continued deeper into the woods to a camp site.

They were still in New Mexico. Mario had decided not to cross the border. Most of the gang members did not have passports, and trying to cross the border would draw too much attention to the gang. Mario had made arrangements to have the merchandise delivered to him on this side of the border. Mario had the gang set up camp to wait for the delivery.

Mario called and alerted his contact to their arrival. His contact said he would be there in about an hour. He and his friends had already slipped across the border and had been waiting for Mario's call.

The gang members started making camp. Some of them made a campfire and started a pot of soup. There was a nearby water source. The water had been piped in for campers. They soon had a large pot of soup cooking thanks to contributions from different gang members. The pouches each contributed mixed into a nice smelling pot of soup.

Another member made some campfire cornbread to go with the soup. As soon as the soup was ready, the guys brought forward their small bowls to be filled. They soon finished up with the soup and the cornbread. After cleaning all of their dishes and pans and packing them away, several of the guys started a card game. They had barely gotten started when they heard the sound of an engine coming. The guys were quickly on the alert.

Two trucks pulled into the campsite. The trucks stopped and the men got out. They had two young girls with them. Their leader went over to talk with Mario. He motioned Mario to follow him to the back of the truck. The leader lifted a tarp and showed Mario the bricks of drugs. He covered the drugs up, and he and Mario moved away from everyone to talk.

The leader was saying something to Mario and Mario was shaking his head. Mario looked over at the girls and looked uncertain. Finally, he shrugged and nodded.

Mario handed a package of money to the leader and came

over and told the gang to start loading the drugs into their saddlebags. The gang members started loading up the drugs.

Mario came over to Sling Shot and Leon. "Part of the deal was to take these two girls to their relatives in the states. Sling Shot, one can ride behind you. Dazzler, you can take the other. I expect you two to take good care of them. Keep them away from the other guys."

"Sure thing, Boss," said Sling Shot.

Leon took his spare helmet and showed one of the girls how to wear it. When Sling Shot saw what Leon was doing, he helped the other girl to wear his spare helmet. Leon helped a girl to sit on the back of his bike and Sling Shot helped the other onto his bike.

They were about to mount their bikes when a voice through a megaphone called out.

"This is the Police. Everyone freeze, you are under arrest."

There was immediate gunfire from the gang and the drug dealers. Leon grabbed both girls and pulled them down between his and Sling Shot's bikes and tried to cover them with his body. When Sling Shot saw what he was doing, he covered the girls, too. There was gunfire everywhere. All Leon and Sling Shot could do was stay down and hope not to get hit.

Finally, the gunfire ceased. Leon looked around slowly and then checked Sling Shot and the girls. They seemed to be alright.

"Hold it right there," said a Fed. He had a gun pointed at him, so Leon raised his hands. Sling Shot did likewise. They stood still and didn't move or say anything.

The Fed reached over and roughly pulled one of the girls up. "What are you doing here?" he asked. The girl had no idea what he was asking. She did not speak English. The Fed gave her a shake and repeated the question. The girl started to cry.

Leon looked at the Fed. "If you hurt this girl one more time, I will see to it you are kicked off the force," he said in a stern no-nonsense voice.

The Fed turned toward Leon and started to raise his gun on him. Morris came up behind him. "I wouldn't do that if I were you," said Morris.

The Fed turned and stared at Morris. "Mr. Morris," he stammered.

"Since when do you threaten my agents?" asked Morris.

"I didn't know he was an agent," said the Fed.

"We don't mistreat young women, either," said Leon.

"What about him?" asked the Fed, motioning to Sling Shot.

"He's not part of this," said Leon. "He is helping me take these two girls to their family."

Sling Shot didn't say anything, but he did relax a little.

Morris looked at Leon and Sling Shot. "These two are working for me. Go round up any others you haven't shot already." He waited until the Fed was gone before speaking to Leon. "What are you up to?" he asked Leon.

"I'm calling in a favor you owe me for keeping Glenda and my baby hidden from me." Leon nodded at Morris's surprised look. "Yeah, I know about it. I was going to beat the crap out of you, but if you leave Sling Shot and the girls for me to take care of, I'll give you a pass this time."

"You will be responsible for him," said Morris.

"Yes, he won't get into any more trouble," said Leon.

Morris turned and left. "By the way," Leon called. Morris turned and looked back at him. "Both my wife and I are out of your department. We quit," said Leon.

"You're wife?" asked Morris.

"Yes, my wife, Glenda," said Leon.

Morris nodded. "So, that's why we couldn't find her."

"You had better be glad you didn't find her or the whole Indian nation would have been after you. There would have been nowhere you could hide where we could not find you," stated Leon. Morris hurried away.

Leon turned to Sling Shot. "You ready to ride?" he asked. He stopped and looked at Sling Shot. "I didn't ask if you wanted to go with me."

"Yes," said Sling Shot seriously. "I'll go whereever you lead." Leon laughed.

"Are we to go with you?" asked one of the girls.

Leon looked at the girl. She was speaking a dialect he understood. "If you want to," answered Leon in the same dialect.

"They were planning to sell us as prostitutes. They said if we tried to run away they would kill our families. We can not go back. We have nowhere else to go," she said.

"We will help you. You are not going to be sold. Do you want to go with us?" asked Leon. The girls looked at each other and nodded.

Leon and Sling Shot loaded them onto the back of their bikes and climbed on and started for the Indian reservation and home.

CHAPTER 13

*L*eon stopped at a motel on the edge of the town where he and Sling Shot had bought food when they were camped out the first night. He rented two rooms, each with two double beds. One room was for the girls and one was for him and Sling Shot. They went to the same fast food place to eat before going to their rooms to sleep.

"Where are we headed, Dazzler?" asked Sling Shot as they lay down to rest.

"My name is Leon Black Feather," said Leon. "What is your name?"

"My name is Hugh Haynes," said Sling Shot.

"Well, Hugh, since Morris made me responsible for you, I guess you will have to come to the reservation with me. Do you know anything about horses?"

"Yes, I worked on a ranch in Texas for awhile. I liked working there, but the owner went bankrupt, and I had to move on,"

"My brothers and I own a place where we raise horses. We train them and sell them to the rodeo circuit. If you want to work for us, I'll see what I can work out," said Leon.

"I'd like to try it out. Being around horses is better than being around people sometimes," said Hugh.

"What are we going to do with the girls?" asked Hugh.

"I'm not sure," said Leon. "One of them told me they did not have family in the states. She said they were stolen and were being sold as prostitutes. The men told them if they ran away their families would be killed. They are afraid to go back and they are afraid for their families," said Leon.

"Wow," said Hugh. "That sure does complicate things."

"I'll figure something out," said Leon.

Leon's phone rang. He looked at the screen before answering.

"Hi, Dad, is Glenda alright?"

"She's fine. Moon Walking told me to call you. She told me you were on your way home. She said to tell you to bring the girls to her. She asked me to look into bringing their families up to the reservation. She said we could get permission to bring our cousins to the reservation to live. We have to work fast and quietly before anyone knows we are getting them out of harm's way. Oh, she also said the young man will do well working with the horses," said Glen.

Leon burst out laughing. "We can always depend on Moon Walking. Is Glenda there, Dad?"

"Yes, she is, hold on."

"Hello," said Glenda.

"Hi, how's my girl?" asked Leon.

"I'm doing great, now I can talk to you. Are you really on your way home?" she asked.

"Yes, I should be there tomorrow. I love you," said Leon. "I told Morris we quit. I don't think we will have any more problems with him. I'll tell you all about it when I see you. Is the baby okay?" asked Leon.

"Your son is fine. He can't wait to see his daddy. I know

how he feels. I love you. I'm glad we are done with Morris."

"Yes, so am I. Good night, I love you," said Leon.

Leon and Glenda hung up the phones and Leon looked at Hugh, grinning at him from the other bed. "Dad is making arrangements to bring the girls' families to the reservation, hopefully before the kidnappers find out about it. It is all arranged for you to work with the horses," said Leon with a laugh.

"How did he find out about all of that? I was right here. I did not hear you tell him anything," said Hugh

Leon laughed. "You are in for a treat. You are going to meet Moon Walking. She is our tribe's wise woman and an elder. She always knows what is going on. She told my dad earlier today to start the paperwork to rescue the girls' families. She also said you are going to love working with the horses," said Leon.

"Well, I'll be," said Hugh as he turned over and tried to sleep.

Leon grinned. "I'm going home to Glenda and my son," he thought. He closed his eyes and slept.

The next morning Leon checked them out of their rooms and took them back to the fast food place to eat before getting on the road again. While they were eating, he asked the girls their names.

"My name is Leia and she is Meri," said the girl who did all of the talking. Meri was too shy to talk much.

Leon smiled at the girls. "My name is Leon Black Feather, and this is Hugh Haynes. Our tribal elder said to bring you to her. She is going to find you a place to live while we are trying to bring your families to the reservation."

Leia interrupted him. "You are going to bring our families here?" she asked.

"We are going to try," said Leon. "Moon Walking seemed

to think it was possible."

"Moon Walking," said Leia. "You know Moon Walking?"

Leon looked at her curiously. "Yes, do you?"

"I have heard many tales about her from my Madre. She is my Madre's third cousin. I found it hard to believe all the stories Madre told about Moon Walking," said Leia.

"I don't know what you heard, but it is probably all true. Moon Walking is a legend in her own time," said Leon.

Leia shook her head and turned to Meri. "Moon Walking is going to take care of us and bring our families out," she said. Meri smiled at Leon and Hugh.

"We had better get going," said Leon. "We still have a long trip ahead of us. They all walked out to the bikes and the girls eagerly put on their helmets and climbed onto the back of the bikes. Leon shook his head and grinned at Hugh. "Let's head home," he said.

Hugh grinned back and gave him a thumbs-up before starting his bike and heading out with Leon beside him.

They made good time. They only stopped once to eat and fill up with gas and go to the bathroom. Leon made a detour around Rolling Fork and took a road leading straight to the reservation. It was around four when Leon stopped at the gate of the reservation. He smiled and took off his helmet when Don Small Eagle and Tim Little Eagle blocked the gate.

"Hi, guys," said Leon grinning.

"Leon," greeted Don. He reached out to shake Leon's hand. "I'm glad to see you back. Congratulations on your marriage and the baby."

"Thank you, I don't think you are going to have to worry about trespassers as much now. I am not sure how many of the gang survived the shoot out; but the ones alive are on their way to jail. It should make things easier around here for awhile," said Leon.

"We'll hang around until the head of security tells us to go. I'm sure he will let us know soon," said Tim. "Moon Walking left a message for you. She said to bring the girls by the offices at the Sports Complex."

"Okay," said Leon, starting his bike and putting on his helmet. "I better not keep Moon Walking waiting."

He nodded to Don and Tim and led the way to the Sports Complex near the school. When they arrived at the Sports Complex, there were several cars parked out front. Leon recognized one as his dad's. He and Hugh helped the girls off the bikes and attached the spare helmets to the back of their bikes. Leon led the way inside. He spotted his dad sitting with Moon Walking and Black Bear, another elder, at a table close to the back of the building. Leon made his way toward them with Hugh and the girls following.

His dad and Moon Walking rose when they approached. Black Bear remained seated.

Leon clasped his dad's hand and smiled at him. He turned to Moon Walking and smiled. "Moon Walking, I want to thank you for all of your help, especially with my wedding. I want to say you are truly a blessing to everyone in this tribe." Leaning forward, Leon kissed her cheek.

Moon Walking smiled at Leon. "Glen," she said. "You and Daisy have raised one smooth talker." Everyone smiled at this statement.

"Now, about the girls, Glen has already drawn up papers for Judge Hawthorn to sign stating the girls' families may come to the reservation. We just have to get the Feds approval and we can bring them to the reservation."

Leon took out his phone and dialed Morris.

"Hello, Leon, I didn't think I would be hearing from you again," said Morris.

"I have a request from Moon Walking. She is trying to

bring some cousins of hers to the reservation. She is afraid they may be in danger in Mexico. She has Judge Hawthorn's approval. I was wondering if you know anyone to help her."

"Yeah, I guess I owe you for not beating the crap out of me. I'll talk to someone and have them send approval to Judge Hawthorn. He can fax approval to the head of security's office. You should have it within the hour," said Morris. "You are not going to make a habit of this, are you?"

"No, I won't make a habit of it. Thanks, Morris." Leon hung up the phone and grinned at Moon Walking and Glen. "He is having someone send approval to Judge Hawthorne. Judge Hawthorn will fax approval for the families to be allowed to come to the reservation. It should be at the security office within the hour."

Glen laughed. "How did you manage to get him to agree?" he asked.

"He probably didn't want Leon to beat the crap out of him," said Hugh.

Leon laughed and turned to Hugh. "Moon Walking, Dad, this is Hugh Haynes. He is going to be helping with the horses."

"Pleased to meet you," said Hugh. "It has been a real education getting to know Leon." Everyone laughed at this truth.

Leon drew the girls forward. He spoke in the dialect they understood to introduce them. He knew Moon Walking and his dad also understood the dialect.

"Moon Walking, this is Leia and Meri. Girls, this is Moon Walking."

Leia stepped forward and gazed at Moon Walking in awe.

"My Madre has told me so many stories about the great Moon Walking," said Leia.

Moon Walking clasped Leia's hand. "I have arranged for

you to stay with my grandson and granddaughter while we wait for your families to arrive," she said.

"They are really coming?" asked Leia with tears in her eyes.

"We are going to do our best to see them all safely with us," said Moon Walking.

"Thank you," said Leia.

"Thank you, also, Leon and Hugh, for bringing us here," said Leia. Meri nodded her agreement.

Moon Walking turned to Glen. "Will you take the girls to Little Flower? She is waiting on their arrival. She will take care of them."

"Yes, after I drop them off, I will go by security and pick up the fax," said Glen.

"We will then have to arrange for someone to go and pick up the families before they are harmed," said Moon Walking. Moon Walking waved him on. "We can discuss the plan after we get the papers," she said. Glen left, taking the girls to Little Flower.

Leon and Hugh followed him out of the building and said goodbye to the girls.

"Where to next?' asked Hugh.

"Now, I take you to my brother Marcel. He has a bunkhouse where you can stay while we get you started in your new job. We all are partners in raising the horses, but he is the only one with a bunkhouse," said Leon.

"Lead on," said Hugh. Leon laughed and started his bike in the direction of their land with Hugh following.

Marcel came out when he heard the motorcycles. He grinned big when he recognized Leon. When Leon and Hugh stopped in front of Marcel's porch, Marcel met Leon with a smile and a hug. "Leon, boy, am I glad to see you. I know someone else who will be glad to see you, too," said Marcel with a smile.

"It's good to finally be home for good," said Leon.

"You're done with the Feds? Great!" said Marcel. "You ready to start helping with the horses?" asked Marcel.

"Yes," agreed Leon. "I brought you some more help, too. Marcel, this is Hugh. I told him he could work with the horses."

Marcel held out his hand. "Good to meet you, Hugh. We will be happy to let you join us."

"I figure being with the horses will be tame compared to being around Leon," drawled Hugh.

Marcel shook Hugh's hand and laughed with him. Marcel looked at Leon and smiled. "He has you pegged, Bro," said Marcel.

Leon just shook his head. "I'll see you all later. I have a wife waiting for me at home." He started his bike and headed for home.

He spotted Glenda as soon as he was close to the house. She was sitting on the porch with Daisy. When she saw Leon coming, she left her seat and made her way down the steps. She was standing at the bottom of the steps when Leon stopped his bike. He took off his helmet and laid it on his seat and started toward Glenda.

Glenda started walking toward him, and he started running to reach her. Leon and Glenda both were reaching out to hold each other, although Glenda had a little trouble getting close. Leon started kissing her. They kissed until they had to stop to breathe.

Daisy turned and went inside to give them a little more privacy. Jamie and Silas found something to do around the other side of the house.

"I am so glad you are here and we don't have to report to

Morris any more," said Glenda. She was putting small kisses all over his face.

"We could go inside," said Leon.

"I don't want to move," said Glenda. "I'm afraid I'll wake up and find out it's all another dream."

"If you are dreaming, I'm dreaming with you. We are going to be living this dream for a long time," said Leon kissing her again.

He lifted her up and carried her up the steps and to the door.

"Leon, put me down. I'm too heavy for you to carry," said Glenda.

"You're not heavy. You're perfect," said Leon, opening the door with a push and carrying her inside. He carried her over to the sofa and sat down with her in his lap.

He held her close and proceeded to continue kissing her. Leon felt a hard bump against his hand as it was resting on her baby bump.

"Ah, our little one doesn't want to be ignored," grinned Leon.

Glenda laughed. "He's very active. I have a feeling he's going to take after his dad," said Glenda.

"I can hardly wait," said Leon.

"It won't be much longer," said Glenda. "The midwife said it could happen anytime in the next couple of weeks. She said he is very impatient."

"I am glad I made it back in time. I am sorry I have not been around to see you through the pregnancy," said Leon.

"It was not your fault. You didn't know," said Glenda. "You are here, now. You will be here when your son is born."

"Yes, I will," agreed Leon. He held her close and said a thank you to the Great Spirit for bringing such blessings into his life.

CHAPTER 14

*A*fter Glen dropped the girls off to a waiting Little Flower, otherwise known as Angelica, he went by and picked up the fax from Roy Hawk at the security office. Glen looked over the papers. They were all in order. It gave them permission to send two Native Americans to pick up the families of Moon Walking's cousin. It gave the families permission to live on the reservation, and it was signed by Judge Hawthorn and the Governor. Glen smiled. The Governor must have been visiting Judge Hawthorn.

Roy suggested they send Jamie and Silas to pick up the families. Since the brothers had been to Mexico for Roy, he knew they had passports.

"The gang is under control. Mario was killed in the shootout along with six other members. The remaining three are under arrest. Most of the drug traffickers were also killed," said Roy. "I am going to keep a guard on the gate for a while longer, but with Mark and Leon at home, the family should be safe."

"I'll talk to Jamie and Silas as soon as I get home. The faster we can have the families moved, the better," said Glen.

When Glen stopped in front of his home, Jamie and Silas came to meet him. He noticed Leon's bike in front of the house. "I see Leon made it home alright," stated Glen.

"Yes, he is inside," said Silas.

"I'm going to need you two to go down to Mexico and pick up Moon Walking's cousin and her families," said Glen.

"What about guarding the girls?" asked Jamie.

"Most of the gang was killed in a shootout and the rest are in jail. I think Mark and Leon can watch over everyone until you get back," said Glen.

"Roy said you both have passports," said Glen.

"Yes, we do," agreed Jamie.

"You will need two trucks. You are going to be moving two families. We have permission from the governor to bring them to the reservation. You will have to move fast and quietly. They are being threatened, and we want to get to them before they are hurt or killed. They do not speak English, so you will have to be able to speak and understand the dialect. I know you both learned to speak it with Mark and Leon," said Glen

"Yes, Sir, we did," said Silas grinning. "We used to have fun talking around Dawn and Summer. Summer would get so mad when she couldn't understand what we were saying. I think she learned to speak it just so she could listen to what we were saying."

Glen shook his head and grinned. "You two talk to Moon Walking and find out what you need to know. Be careful and call us if you need help. Have a safe trip."

"We will," said Jamie. The guys shook Glen's hand and left to talk to Moon Walking.

Glen turned and went inside. He saw Leon sitting on the sofa with Glenda held close in his arms. He went over and touched him lightly on the shoulder.

Leon opened his eyes and looked at Glen. He glanced down at Glenda sleeping safe in his arms.

"I thought you two would rest better in bed," said Glen softly. "Glenda has the second room on the right at the top of the stairs."

"Okay," said Leon. He eased up, still holding Glenda close and carried her up the stairs. In the bedroom, Leon pulled the covers back and lowered Glenda to the bed. He took off her shoes and her outer clothes, then he covered her with a blanket. After removing his own clothes, Leon pulled the blanket back and climbed into the bed. He covered them both and pulled Glenda close. He kissed her softly and fell asleep with his wife in his arms.

Jamie and Silas went by their home and picked up another truck. They then went to see Moon Walking. Moon Walking was on her porch waiting for them. Jamie and Silas stopped in front of Moon Walking's house and went to the porch to talk to her.

Moon Walking handed them two letters. One was for Leia's family, and one was for Meri's family. Little Flower had asked each girl to write a letter to her family. They wanted to be sure the families knew the girls were alright and it was safe for them to come with Jamie and Silas. There was also a paper showing the addresses of the families and how to find them.

"Tell the families there is no need to bring furniture. I am having two houses prepared just outside of town. They will be fully furnished," said Moon Walking. "May the Great Spirit watch over you and bring you back safely," Moon Walking told Jamie and Silas.

"Thank you, Moon Walking. We will take good care of your kinfolk," said Silas. Moon Walking nodded regally and watched them enter their trucks and start their journey.

While Jamie and Silas were starting their trip, Mark and

Doris were getting ready to testify at Derrick Bolin's trial. The trial was due to start the next day. The District Attorney asked Mark and Doris to come in and go over a few things with him. Glen decided to go along with them just to make sure there were no loopholes to get Derrick out of serving time.

The three of them entered the District Attorney office and were offered seats.

"This is mostly a formality," said Lance Carlson, the District Attorney. "Mr. Bolin has agreed to plead guilty to a lesser charge. The charge has been lowered to reckless driving instead of attempted vehicular homicide."

"How much time will he get?" asked Glen.

Mark was too angry to talk to the District Attorney.

"He will get ten years, but he could be out in five," stated Lance. "I'm sorry. You will be notified when he comes up for parole. You can appear at his parole hearing and protest him being released. There was nothing I could do about it. It was all settled before I was notified."

"Who pulled this off?" asked Glen.

"I'm told it had to do with Derrick's father pulling strings with a cousin. The cousin is a senator, and he collected on some favors," said Lance.

"So, Derrick Bolin gets away with killing Doris's parents and trying to kill her," said Mark.

"We couldn't prove he killed her parents," said Lance.

"We know he ordered his gang to do it," said Mark. "Well, at least he won't have them to do his bidding anymore. The Feds took care of them."

"Yes, they did," agreed Lance smiling.

"Thank you all for coming in today. Are you going to be at the sentencing tomorrow?" asked Lance.

"Yes, I'll be there. I don't think it is a good idea for him to see Doris. The less he thinks about her, the better," said Mark.

"We'll discuss it later," said Doris.

"Okay," agreed Mark squeezing her hand.

The three of them bid the District Attorney goodbye and left the courthouse. They did not talk on the way to the car. Each of them was too busy with their own thoughts.

They had come in Glen's car. So they took seats in his car for the ride back to the reservation.

"Do you think Hugh or Stanley would know anything about Derrick ordering the hit on Doris's parents?" asked Glen.

Mark straightened and looked at Glen. "I don't know, but we can ask them," said Mark.

When they arrived at the reservation, they drove to Marcel's house.

Marcel was in a side enclosure. He had Stanley with him. They were working with a horse. When Glen pulled to a stop close by, they stopped and came over to the fence. Glen, Mark, and Doris walked over and looked over the fence.

"Nice," said Mark admiring the horse.

"Yeah, he's coming along nicely," said Marcel.

"Hi, Stanley," said Glen.

"Hello. Mr. Black Feather," said Stanley.

"I was wondering, Stanley, when you were with the gang, did you hear anything about Derrick ordering a drive-by shooting?" asked Glen.

"I heard some rumors, but if he ordered anything like that, he would have had Bull and his buddies do it. Those guys were crazy. They did not care who they hurt," said Stanley. "I heard about most of the gang being killed. Is Mario really gone?"

"Yes, he is really gone. The members who were not killed

are being tried in federal court. You should be safe for now. Derrick will be sentenced tomorrow," said Glen.

"Sentenced? Don't they have to try him?" asked Marcel.

"He took a plea bargain," said Mark.

Marcel just shook his head. "How does scum like him get a break like this?" asked Marcel.

"He has a cousin who is a senator. His dad called in some favors," said Mark grimly.

Doris squeezed Mark's hand. She had been holding onto him tightly.

Mark looked down at her, but she was not looking at him. She was staring at the large horse standing beside Marcel.

Mark grinned. "It won't be so bad," he whispered.

"How can you expect me to ride something so big and so far away from the ground?" asked Doris. The other guys, hearing the question, looked at Doris and looked at the large horse she was staring at. They all started smiling.

"The horse you will learn to ride on will be a mare, and she is much smaller," said Glen.

"Doris looked at him in disbelief. "Uh-huh," she said.

"Dad's right. The mare we let learners ride is a sweetheart. You'll love her," said Marcel.

Doris looked over at him in disgust. "You are just trying to get me back for the remark about finding you a wife," said Doris.

"What remark?" asked Mark and Glen, together.

"It was nothing," said Doris waving her hand dismissively, "I was teasing him.

"I wasn't trying to get back at you," said Marcel. "Come up to the barn and I'll introduce you to Sadie. You'll see I'm telling you the truth."

Doris still looked uncertain, but she held tightly to Mark's hand as they followed Marcel to the barn. They left Stanley and Glen down at the fence talking and went into the barn, and Marcel led them to Sadie's stall. Sadie stuck her head through the front and gazed at Doris with big brown eyes.

"Ohhhh," said Doris rubbing the sot nose Sadie was thrusting into her hand.

"Here," said Marcel, handing her a piece of apple. "She likes a treat," said Marcel as Doris took the apple and held it out for Sadie to eat.

Doris continued to pet and talk soothingly to Sadie a little longer. "Do you think we have given Glen enough time to talk to Stanley?" asked Doris softly.

Mark and Marcel looked at her in astonishment. "You mean you were just putting on to give Dad time to talk to Stanley by himself?" asked Mark.

Marcel was grinning. "Smart," said Marcel.

"Well, all of us there at one time were making Stanley nervous. He probably felt like we were ganging up on him," said Doris. Doris took Mark's arm and led the way back outside.

"Did you meet Sadie?" asked Glen.

"Yes," agreed Doris. "She is a real sweetheart."

"We need to get on home and see if there is any word from Jamie and Silas," said Glen.

They said goodbye to Marcel and Stanley and headed for home.

Daisy was busy gathering things to help in furnishing the two houses for Moon Walking's cousins.

"Moon Walking has some ladies cleaning the houses. Some of the men are cutting the grass and straightening the yards. Other ladies are hanging curtains. Everyone on the reservation is donating furniture and supplies. A lot of them are dropping things off at the Sports Complex and the teenagers are carrying it over to the houses. Everyone is rushing to make sure these families have what they need to survive until they get settled and find work," said Daisy.

"What can we do to help?" asked Doris.

"Well, Glen and Mark can take the truck and take these spare beds and linens over to the houses," said Daisy.

Mark and Glen started loading the truck while Doris rounded up sheets and towels.

Mark and Glen took the load over to the houses so they could help each other unload.

Daisy had asked Mark to bring down the cradle from the attic while they were getting the beds. She had him put the cradle in the dining room to be cleaned. While Mark and Glen were gone, Doris gave the cradle a good cleaning.

Daisy looked at the cradle with satisfaction. "It looks as good as new," she said.

"Was this your cradle?" asked Doris.

"Yes, Glen made it for me when I was expecting Leon. Every one of my children used it. Now, Leon's son will use it," she said.

"It's beautiful," said Glenda coming into the dining room and seeing the cradle.

"Yes, it is," agreed Leon as he followed her into the room. He did not seem to want to be far from her since he had returned.

Glenda smiled at Leon and leaned back into his arms.

"Leon, why don't you take the cradle up to your room?" asked Daisy.

"Okay, Mom." Leon helped Glenda into a chair, and then he picked up the cradle and carried it upstairs.

It took Glen and Mark a little longer to drop off their load than they expected. Moon Walking put them to work carrying other furniture in and placing it where she decided it belonged.

By the time they made it back, Daisy and Doris had supper on the table while Sarah and Orin had done their homework. When they finished their homework, they went into the living room to play a video game.

After supper was eaten and the kitchen was cleaned, Doris and Mark went out to sit on the porch.

They sat in their favorite seat. Mark sat in a rocking chair with Doris in his lap.

"I have been thinking about Derrick's sentencing. I think you are right about me not going. Derrick doesn't need to see me. It might feed his obsession. Maybe, if he doesn't see me, he will fixate on someone else, someone who wants him back," said Doris.

"We can hope," said Mark.

Leon and Glenda joined them on the porch. He sat in a rocker and pulled Glenda into his lap. Glenda smiled up at him and relaxed against him. Leon kissed her lightly. He relaxed back with a sigh. He was right where he wanted to be.

Glen came out and claimed the last rocker.

"Moon Walking called. She heard from Jamie and Silas. They are close to the border, but they are going to rest tonight and go across first thing in the morning. They thought it would be easier to find their way in the daylight," Glen leaned back and looked up at the stars.

Daisy came out and Glen caught her hand and pulled her into his lap.

Daisy Laughed. "The boys are teaching you bad habits," she said.

"Who do you think we learned them from?" asked Mark.

They all laughed. They were enjoying holding their loved ones in their arms and gazing at the stars.

～

The next morning, Mark and Glen went to Rolling Fork to attend Derrick's sentencing. They sat in the courtroom and watched Derrick being brought in. He was in handcuffs. When Derrick was brought into the room, he stopped and looked around. He frowned as the bailiff had him to sit. He had been looking for Doris. Mark was sure of it. Derrick had not recognized him. He had passed right over him when he scanned the courtroom looking for Doris.

The charges were read and Derrick pled guilty. Judge Hawthorn looked around the courtroom. He looked at Mark and Glen and nodded slightly. He looked at Derrick and frowned.

"Will the prisoner rise?" called the bailiff. Derrick's lawyer had him to rise.

"Derrick Bolin, you are charged with reckless driving," said Judge Hawthorn. "How do you plead?"

"Guilty, your honor," said Derrick.

"You will be sentenced to fifteen years. You will have a parole hearing every five years. How soon you are released will be dependent on your behavior. You will be taken immediately to the federal prison to begin your sentence."

Derrick was taken out and Mark and Glen rose to leave. Mark looked at Judge Hawthorn and smiled. The Judge smiled back at him. He and Glen made a quick stop at Captain Michael's office. He was out for the day, so they made their way outside and headed to the reservation.

Doris used the time Mark was gone to work on her bracelet. She finished the star and started on the border. She made quick work of the border. It went together easily. Now all she had left to do was get Daisy to show her how to do the ends.

Doris looked at the bracelet with proud satisfaction. She had made it. She hoped Mark liked it. She heard a car out front and hurriedly put away the bracelet and went downstairs. Mark and Glen were coming in the door.

"How did it go?" asked Doris.

"Better than I expected," said Mark.

"The Judge gave him fifteen years. He could still get out in five, but if he causes any trouble, he will go right back in," said Mark. He gave Doris a hug. "Are you ready to set a date?" he asked.

"Yes," answered Doris.

"How about three weeks from today. We'll have time for the house raising, and Leon's baby should be here by then, so we can all have fun and enjoy the day?" said Mark.

"Are we ready for the house raising?" asked Doris.

"Laughing Elk is almost finished with the basement and flooring. Jamie's cousin has done the plumbing and I have someone ready to do the electrical work. The material is ready to be delivered. I am going to see about having a house raising as soon as Jamie and Silas get back," said Mark.

"It all sounds wonderful," said Doris raising her face for a kiss.

"Where are we going to hold the ceremony?" asked Doris after a very satisfying pause.

"There is a lodge on the reservation. It was built to hold meetings and other ceremonies in. We can ask Moon Walking if it is free," said Mark.

Doris laughed. We are going to have to do something. If anyone else shows up, I don't know where your folks will put them."

Mark smiled. "Mom will manage. She loves a full house. She misses us when we are all away."

"Yeah, I know, she looks like she is really enjoying the crowd," said Doris.

Mark pulled his ringing phone out of his pocket to answer.

"Hello."

"Hello, Mark, I wanted to let you know. Silas and I have both families and are back across the border. We should be in late tonight. Will you let Moon Walking know for me?" asked Jamie.

"Sure, I'll call her, but she probably already knows," laughed Mark.

"Yeah," laughed Jamie.

"Be careful and call me if you need me," said Mark.

"I will, thanks," said Jamie.

Mark hung up and called Moon Walking.

"Hello, Mark," said Moon Walking.

"Jamie called. They are back across the border and have both families. They should be here late tonight."

"Yes, thank you. We will be ready."

Moon Walking hung up, and Mark grinned down at Doris.

"Now, where were we?" he asked, pulling her close for another kiss.

Daisy came in, and Mark turned and smiled at her.

"Jamie and Silas are on their way back," he said.

"Good," said Daisy.

"I was thinking of having the house raising this coming weekend," said Mark.

"I have been thinking," said Daisy. "Why don't you wait another week or so on the house raising. Get everything done you can beforehand. It will take two day's work on a house as big as yours. We can set up and have your wedding at the house site at the end of the second day of work. It will be a short day. Everyone will already be there and it will be a nice way to say thank you for all of their help."

"What a great idea!" Doris exclaimed. "I like the idea of being married in our new house."

"It would be a great way to christen our new house," grinned Mark.

He went over and hugged Daisy. "Thanks, Mom."

Daisy hugged him back and smiled at Doris.

"Do you need any help with your bracelet?" she asked.

"Yes, I need you to help me with the ends," said Doris.

"What?" said Mark. "You are almost done. I had better get busy and finish mine."

Doris grinned at him. "I didn't know what I was doing. I wanted to give myself plenty of time."

Daisy and Doris went over to help get the houses ready for the families. Glen had gone and picked up Leia and Meri and taken them to the houses to help and to await the arrival of their families.

When Jamie called to let them know the trucks were almost there, Mark went to the gate to wait for them and guide them to the houses. He was also going to help Jamie and Silas unload. He knew they would be weary from the trip.

The gate guards waved the trucks on through when they arrived, and Mark pulled out in front to guide them. When they stopped in front of the houses, there was a large crowd to welcome them. Moon Walking and the girls came forward to welcome them first. The girls were very excited to see their families again. When they had been taken, they thought they would not see them again. When Moon Walking greeted her cousin, it was amazing how much they resembled each other.

"Welcome to your new home," said Moon Walking.

"Thank you, Moon Walking. My Madre told me many stories about you and the reservation. I am very happy to be here," said her cousin.

As soon as they had the new residents settled in their new homes, the people started leaving a few at a time. Jamie and Silas left to get some much-needed sleep. Mark took Doris and left for home. Daisy left with Glen.

They all went to bed and to sleep as soon as they arrived home.

Moon Walking explained about some of the modern things in the houses. The place where the families came from had been very primitive. After showing them the refrigerator full of food and the stove, Moon Walking said good night. Her cousin came forward and thanked her again and hugged her.

Moon Walking looked up at the stars as she noticed someone waiting for her outside. "Little Bear, what are you doing here?"

"I waited to give you a ride home. I know you must be very weary. You look after everyone else, Moon Walking. Come on, relax and let me take care of you for once."

Moon Walking settled into the car seat with a sigh. It felt good to let someone else take care of her for once.

The first day of building went well. The men were working well together, and the ladies were setting up the food. The children were running around playing and somehow staying out of the way of the men. The new families had joined in. The men were able builders and had already been offered jobs with Laughing Elk's uncle.

The walls were going up fast, and the electrician was

working on the inside as soon as a wall was finished. At the end of the day, everyone went home tired but happy. They were all looking forward to the wedding the next day.

Doris had found the perfect dress. It had to be sleeveless because of the bracelet. Mark could not wear a suit. He had to wear short sleeves.

Daisy had offered her dress to Doris, but Doris had told her to keep it for Summer. Doris explained she wanted a dress she could keep and pass down to her daughters. Daisy understood and got a little misty-eyed at the thought of more granddaughters.

Orin and Sarah had new outfits. They were going to bring the bracelets down at the ceremony.

After lunch on the second day, some of the men set up an open tent and put out some folding chairs for the older people to sit in. Doris had gone to Dawn's house to change. Sarah had gone with her to change her own clothes.

More food had been brought to eat after the wedding. The celebration could last well into the night.

Some of the guys had made a stage for the bride and groom to stand on along with Little Bear.

Mark and Orin went inside the house to wash off and change clothes.

Mark and Doris had chosen to have one attendant each. Marcel was standing up for Mark and Dawn was standing up for Doris. Leon did not want to be far from Glenda and Summer was sitting with Daisy. Glen was going to escort Doris to the front.

Everything went as planned. They said their vows and exchanged rings. Little Bear called for the bracelets.

Sarah and Orin came forward, walking side by side. They each held a small pillow with a bracelet in the center. Little Bear picked up Mark's bracelet and handed it to him. Mark took the bracelet and tied it on Doris's arm. It was on a blue background. There was a heart at the bottom and a streak of lightning zig-zagged down the center and ended in the heart.

"You are lightning striking deep into my heart to show me a forever love."

Doris smiled mistily at him as he spoke the words. Then Little Bear handed Doris her bracelet. She tied it onto Mark's arm. It was three colors of blue. Each section was a darker shade. There was a sun at the top, a star in the center, and a moon at the bottom.

"Mark Black Feather, you are the sun to make my world bright, the star to bring a sparkle to my eyes, and the moon who fills my night with love."

There were many misty eyes when Doris finished speaking. Mark leaned in and kissed her.

Little Bear held up his hand and said, "Not yet." Several people laughed. Mark just smiled down at Doris.

Little Bear waited for quiet before speaking. "We ask the Great Spirit to bless these bracelets and the couple wearing them. May the love they weaved into them grow stronger as the years pass. Now, you may kiss the bride." Mark wasted no time following his instructions.

They were interrupted by a loud cry of pain. Everyone looked at Leon and Glenda. She was bent forward in pain and holding tightly to Leon. Daisy hurried to her side, as did the midwife, who was attending the wedding. "We need to get her inside and fix something for her to lie on," said the midwife. "We don't have time to take her anywhere."

Daisy stood and faced the crowd. "Alright, everyone, we need some blankets to make a pallet. We are fixing to have a baby. He wants to join the celebration."

They laughed but hurried to help. Silas came forward with a blow-up mattress. I don't like sleeping on the ground," explained Silas.

"Thank you," said Daisy. "Blow it up for me."

"Yes, Ma'am," said Silas. He took the mattress and soon had it full of air. He carried it to the door and passed it inside. Doris took it over and laid it by the pallet where Glenda was lying.

Leon picked up Glenda and held her while the blankets were placed on the mattress. He then lay her on the mattress just in time for another contraction. She held his hand tightly while she went through it.

It was only a few minutes before their son slid into the arms of his father. The crowd outside heard the loud cry of the baby. There were a lot of smiles and sighs of relief.

Moon Walking stood close to the door of the house. "It is good. This house has been blessed with two new beginnings. Mark and Doris have brought love to it, and Lane Black Feather will lead our tribe into the future."

Inside Leon smiled as he watched Glenda holding their son. "I think Moon Walking just named our son," he said.

Glenda smiled. "What did she name him?" she asked.

"Lane Black Feather."

"Lane Black Feather," she said softly. "I like it."

THE END

Dear reader,

We hope you enjoyed reading *Love's Obsession*. Please take a moment to leave a review in Amazon, even if it's a short one. Your opinion is important to us.

Discover more books by Betty McLain at https://www.nextchapter.pub/authors/betty-mclain

Want to know when one of our books is free or discounted for Kindle? Join the newsletter at http://eepurl.com/bqqB3H

Best regards,

Betty McLain and the Next Chapter Team

The story continues in:
Love's Memory by Betty McLain

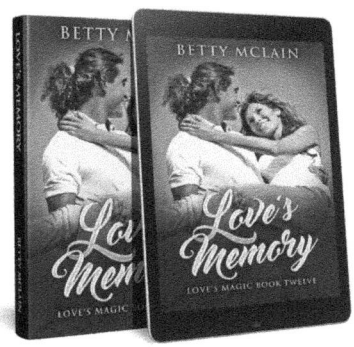

To read the first chapter for free, head to:
https://www.nextchapter.pub/books/loves-memory

ABOUT THE AUTHOR

With five children, ten grandchildren and six great-grandchildren, I have a very busy life, but reading and writing have always been a very large and enjoyable part of my life. I have been writing since I was very young. I kept notebooks with my stories in them private. I didn't share them with anyone. They were all handwritten because I was unable to type. We lived in the country, and I had to do most of my writing at night. My days were busy helping with my brothers and sister. I also helped Mom with the garden and canning food for our family. Even though I was tired, I still managed to get my thoughts down on paper at night.

When I married and began raising my family, I continued writing my stories while helping my children through school and into their own lives and families. My sister was the only one to read my stories. She was very encouraging. When my youngest daughter started college, I decided to go to college myself. I had taken my GED at an earlier date and only had to take a class to pass my college entrance tests. I passed with flying colors and even managed to get a partial scholarship. I took computer classes to learn typing. The English and literature classes helped me to polish my stories.

I found public speaking was not for me. I was much more comfortable with the written word, but researching and writing the speeches was helpful. I could use information to build a story. I still managed to put my own spin on the essays.

I finished college with an associate degree and a 3.4 GPA. I had several awards, including President's List, Dean's List, and Faculty List. The school experience helped me gain more confidence in my writing. I want to thank my English teacher in college for giving me more confidence in my writing by telling me that I had a good imagination. She said I told an interesting story. My daughter, who is a very good writer and has books of her own published, convinced me to have some of my stories published. She used her experience self-publishing to publish my stories them for me. The first time I held one of my books in my hands and looked at my name on it as author, I was so proud. They were very well received. This was encouragement enough to convince me to continue writing and publishing. I have been building my library of books written by Betty McLain since then. I also wrote and illustrated several children's books.

Being able to type my stories opened up a whole new world for me. Having access to a computer helped me to look up anything I needed to know and expanded my ability to keep writing my books. Joining Facebook and making friends all over the world expanded my outlook considerably. I was able to understand many different lifestyles and incorporate them in my ideas.

I have heard the saying, "Watch out what you say, and don't make the writer mad, you may end up in a book being eliminated." It is true. All of life is there to stimulate your imagination. It is fun to sit and think about how a thought can be changed to develop a story and to watch the story develop and come alive in your mind. When I get started, the stories almost write themselves; I just have to get all of it down as I think it before it is gone.

I love knowing the stories I have written are being read

and enjoyed by others. It is awe-inspiring to look at the books and think, "I wrote that."

I look forward to many more years of putting my stories out there and hope the people reading my books are looking forward to reading them as much.